# THE FIFTH SENSE

## A PARANORMAL WOMEN'S FICTION ROMANCE NOVEL

MICHELLE M. PILLOW

MICHELLEPILLOW.COM

*Some secrets refuse to stay buried.*

By all rights, Sue Jewel should be dead. In place of celebrating her fortieth birthday, she was wrapped in plastic and stuffed in the trunk of a car. Worst part is the man she promised to spend her life with is the one who tried to kill her. With a little help from Fate, Sue walks away from the ordeal, but her husband doesn't.

Now with a new lease on life, Sue wants to put as much mileage between her past and her present as she can. It would be a lot easier if something supernatural with dark intent wasn't along for the ride. Desperate to break free from it all, she finds herself in Freewild Cove, making new friends, catching the eye of the handsome coffee shop owner, and hoping to magically cut her ties to her would-be murderer once and for all.

Lorna, Vivien, and Heather are back. And with the help of Grandma Julia's ghost, they're kicking supernatural butt and taking names!

ORDER OF MAGIC SERIES

Second Chance Magic
Third Time's A Charm
The Fourth Power
The Fifth Sense
The Sixth Spell

Visit MichellePillow.com for details!

*To my husband, John.*
*Thank you for all you do.*
*I love you.*

# AUTHOR NOTE

Being an author in my 40s, I am thrilled to be a part of this Paranormal Women's Fiction #PWF project. Older women kick ass. We know things. We've been there. We are worthy of our own literature category. We also have our own set of issues that we face—empty nests, widows, divorces, menopause, health concerns, etc—and these issues deserve to be addressed and embraced in fiction.

Growing older is a real part of life. Women friendships matter. Women matter. Our thoughts and feelings matter.

If you love this project as much as I do, be sure to spread the word to all your reader friends and let the vendors where you buy your books know you want to see a special category listing on their sites for 40+ heroines in Paranormal Women's Fiction and Romance.

Happy Reading!

Michelle M. Pillow

"Michelle M. Pillow's Second Chance Magic is full of delicious secrets! What's not a secret is how much you're going to love this book and this heroine. I'll take book two now!" - *Kristen Painter, USA TODAY Bestselling Author*

"Delightfully heartfelt and filled with emotion. Psychic powers, newly discovered magic, and a troublesome ex who comes back from the grave. Michelle M. Pillow delivers a wonderfully humorous start to a new paranormal women's fiction romance series." - *Robyn Peterman, NY Times and USA TODAY Bestselling Author*

# CHAPTER ONE

*ST. Louis, Missouri*

The steady beep of a heart monitor let Sue Jewel know she was alive. She focused on her breathing. If she inhaled too deeply, the pain would shoot through her side.

"You're awake." The doctor's smile was perfunctory as his eyes moved to the chart hanging at the end of her bed.

First, the heart monitor let her know she was alive. Now the doctor was informing her she was awake. What was next? Would the nurse come in and confirm she was female?

"This was one heck of a way to spend your fortieth birthday," he continued as if attempting a conversation out of habit rather than the situation.

"How did I get here?" Sue felt nauseous and dizzy and wanted to sleep.

"Ambulance," the doctor answered. "You don't remember the car accident?"

The last thing Sue remembered before blacking out was being kicked in the ribs, then strange flashes of images that looked more nightmare than real.

"No. I don't remember what happened," she lied out of habit.

"That's not unusual after a head injury. The police will want to take a statement later. They'll be able to answer any direct questions you may have." The man's bedside manner was a little cold and clinical, but she preferred it that way.

As the doctor neared, Sue averted her gaze. The painkillers they'd given her helped and, if she didn't make sudden movements and concentrated, she could manage to keep breathing. She welcomed the numbness they offered.

*In. Out. In. Out.*

"Mrs. Jewel?"

Sue glanced at the doctor. He placed a hand on her shoulder, and she flinched. "Did you hear me?"

"Uh, yeah," she muttered, trying delicately to pull away from his hand. "I have a head injury."

His hand didn't leave her. If anything, he pressed more firmly. She stiffened under his touch.

"Mrs. Jewel, there is no easy way to tell you this. I'm sorry to inform you that your husband didn't make it." The doctor patted her shoulder, and she turned mid-pat to avoid the tiny jars to her body.

"Make what?"

"He didn't survive the wreck," the doctor clarified.

Sue didn't speak. She finally looked him in the eye.

"He's dead," the doctor stated when she didn't react.

Sue could see, even in his taciturnity, the reaction the doctor expected from her. The truth was she didn't know what she felt—sadness, relief, pain, grief? She closed her eyes, and a tear slipped over her cheek. Her hands trembled.

"Is there someone we can call for you?" he asked.

"I don't have family," Sue answered. The last thing she wanted was Hank's mother showing up to berate her for surviving in place of her precious son.

"Friends?"

Sue shook her head in denial. "I want to be alone, please."

"I understand. A nurse will be in to check on

you. Push the call button if you need anything." The man gave her another awkward pat on the shoulder. "When you're ready, we have people you can talk to about what happened."

*In. Out. In. Out.*

Sue kept her eyes closed and focused on her breathing, counting them to distract her mind from the pain. She had no idea how much time passed in the marking of those seconds.

*In. Out. In. Out. In...*

"Mrs. Jewel, I'm Detective Price. I'd like to ask you a few questions, if that's all right?"

Sue hadn't heard the detective come in. She debated whether she could pretend to sleep until the man went away. Finally, she opened her eyes and glanced at him. Like the doctor, he looked at her like he was there to do a job, and she was merely part of that job. All she had to do was give him enough answers to make him check all the little boxes on whatever form he needed to fill out.

"I'm sorry, I don't remember anything," Sue said. "The doctor said I have a head injury."

"You don't remember being in the trunk?" a woman's voice interjected.

Sue rolled onto her back as she realized another person was in the room, a second detective if the dark slacks and button-down white shirt were any indications. And, if that wasn't, the shiny badge hanging on her belt was a dead giveaway. The woman tried to give her a sympathetic look, but a hard edge remained behind her eyes.

"This is my partner, Detective Sanchez," Price said.

"Nice to meet you," Sue managed. The words sounded polite, maybe too polite considering the circumstances. It wasn't nice to meet anyone at the moment. She didn't want to be here.

*In. Out. In.*

"Can you tell us how you got in the trunk of your car?" Sanchez asked.

"I don't think I was in the trunk." Sue took a deeper breath, fighting the memory of tight spaces and the feel of a crowbar poking into her ribs as tires sped over asphalt. Lying came easier than it should have.

*In. Out.*

"We believe that when the semi clipped the car and sent it into a tailspin down the ravine, you were thrown from the back of the vehicle," Sanchez continued.

"That doesn't sound right," Sue lied out of habit. Her nose burned with the threat of tears.

"The doctor said I injured my head in the accident."

"Yes, you mentioned that." Price crossed his arms over his chest. "The truck driver said your car drifted into his lane. Skid marks on the road support that. Fingerprints on the steering wheel tell us Hank was driving at the time."

"Then that is probably what happened." Sue shook her head. "I don't remember."

"That's not surprising." Sanchez held up her phone to show a picture of a wrecked silver sedan at the bottom of a ravine. The vehicle looked totaled. How Sue survived was anyone's guess. The top had been caved in and the sides were smashed liked crumbled tinfoil. "We found evidence that you were in the trunk when this happened."

"Evidence?" Sue glanced at them before looking at her hands on the thin hospital blanket. Medical tape held the IV against her skin, hiding where it entered her. She followed the tube with her eyes. She willed painkiller oblivion to flow into her body to turn off her mind, but the saline bag only continued to drip in a steady rhythm. A chill worked up her spine, causing her to shiver.

"Blood and hair on the latch," Sanchez continued. "The theory is you hit your head when you flew out."

"That's *one* theory," Price corrected, indicating he had a different mindset.

Sue touched her head, feeling a bandage wrapped around it like a convalescent's crown.

"Anything you can remember could help us understand what happened tonight," Sanchez insisted.

"It sounds like you already know what happened. We had an accident. I broke my ribs." Sue cradled her stomach. "The painkillers they gave me... I don't feel well. I think I'm going to be sick."

"What is the last thing you remember?" Sanchez asked.

"Having dinner with Hank," Sue said. Tears slid from her eyes as she closed them. "He..."

What could she say? The words struggled to push past her tightening throat.

"He didn't make it." She repeated the doctor's phrasing.

*Dead. Hank died.*

"I think we have all we need for now," Price said.

Sanchez clearly disagreed. She approached the bed. "Mrs. Jewel." The detective took a deep breath and gave her a serious stare. "Sue, if your husband did something to you, you need to tell us. He can't hurt you anymore."

"My husband is dead." Her voice was weak. More tears streamed down her face. The words felt foreign and thick on her tongue. "He died."

The stuttered breath felt like a punch in the side. She doubled over and curled her body into a ball.

"Please leave," Sue begged. "It was an accident. A horrible accident. I don't know what you think you found in the trunk, but it's not from tonight."

"My card," Sanchez said. "If you think of anything."

Sue listened to them leave. She reached for a call button and hit it several times. When a nurse entered, she muttered, "Something for the pain. Please. Something for the pain."

She didn't want to feel anymore.

*In. Out. In. Out.*

Blessed numbness came through her IV, and she let it take her into oblivion.

# CHAPTER TWO

*THREE MONTHS LATER...*

It started with the smell of Hank's cologne, a mix of gun oil and cedar, lingering in the bedroom. Sue couldn't shake the feeling of him standing behind her, watching, judging. In those moments, she forgot he was dead.

She donated his clothing and toiletries to charity, hoping that would erase the scent. Then she caught whiffs of it in the middle of the night, waking her from a troubled sleep. She thought it was the pillows, a haunting scent embedded in the polyester filling, so she threw out the pillows, bought new ones, and then shampooed the mattress with the carpet cleaner.

The smell returned.

It showed up in the kitchen and living room, so she cleaned the house ceiling to floor. Nothing helped. The cologne followed her like a cloud when she walked to the grocery store. Flowers emitted a hint of bourbon with their fragrant petals to cause a wave of sickening sweet nausea that forced her to hold her breath whenever she walked past them.

Sue hated going out. People wanted to hug her and tell her how sorry they were for her loss. Even when she could avoid people, every place she went, she was reminded of Hank—mainly because every place smelled like him.

She didn't call the doctor to ask him about it. He'd only want to run more tests, and she'd had enough of the hospital to last a lifetime. Each time someone read her file, their expression would change, and they'd say something about her loss.

Using the homeschool medical degree that was the internet, she checked diagnostic sites for an answer. Olfactory hallucinations were called phantosmia, and head injuries could cause them. After the wreck, that made sense, and there was no big psychological mystery behind why Sue hallucinated Hank.

Sue decided to ignore the smells and hoped they would go away on their own. She rubbed menthol beneath her nose, relying on the overpowering salve to hide the hallucination. The strong scent made her hot tea taste a little funny, but it was better than the alternative.

The flat-screen television's sound played low in the background, its blue-tinted light flashing from the wall as a talk show live-streamed. She sat alone on the couch. An ugly floral lamp she hated cast a soft glow behind her. Actually, she hated most of the decorations. They looked like a pastel flower monster invaded the home and threw up on the walls and furniture. It all reflected the style of Hank's childhood home.

A dirty plate rested on the coffee table next to her purse in the otherwise pristine living room. The half-eaten sandwich had been for sustenance more than flavor. She hadn't felt like cooking.

Seeing her cell phone light up with an incoming call, she didn't pick up. There was only one person who'd be calling, and she didn't want to talk to Hank's mother. Kathy would go on about how wonderful her son was, "an angel, just an absolute angel," and how lucky (with a subtext of undeserving) Sue was to have been married to him. Everyone liked Hank. He was a charming and likable guy. He was the life of the party.

The plastic bag Sue had been avoiding since her

hospital discharge sat on the floor next to her feet. If not for the life insurance check that arrived to remind her of the hospital, she might not have thought to pull it out of the coat closet.

*"Twenty thousand dollars,"* she read before muttering, "wife severance pay."

A wave of grief washed over her as she stared at the numbers so long that they blurred. She wasn't foolish enough to think Hank had bought the policy to take care of her. His motivation would be more so that other people thought he was taking care of her. Appearances had been everything.

Sue pushed aside her teacup, lifted the hospital bag to the table, and reached inside to pull out Detective Sanchez's card. The woman had tried to talk to Sue a couple of times. She had been unable to make a case out of her theories. About a week after the accident, the detective's picture had been in the news in relation to a double homicide investigation.

Sue found a pair of jeans with cuts up the legs from when they'd removed them. Her shirt was missing, and there was blood on the one shoe included in the bag. Sadness and pain clung to them, these everyday objects. She had done her best not to think about the details of that night.

When she started to shove the clothing back into the bag, she noticed an unfamiliar jewelry box inside her shoe. The black-covered chipboard was worn along the edges. Someone at the emergency room had probably dropped it into the wrong bag. She shook the box lightly, hearing the clack of something inside, before opening it.

Sue didn't recognize the tarnished silver ring with delicate engravings. Hank bought her jewelry to wear in front of his friends but nothing like this. Jewelry wasn't her forte, and she wasn't sure if it was an actual antique or just made to look that way. Regardless, whoever had owned it had worn it often. They would probably be missing it.

Sue's attention went to her wedding band with the obnoxious diamond. Most women would have found the size romantic, but Sue knew it for what it was—a giant, shiny warning to other males that she was taken. She pulled the wedding ring off her finger and set it on top of the life insurance check. Her hand looked naked without it, but there was something freeing about knowing she didn't have to slip it back on ever again.

Knowing she should call the hospital to report the mistake with the antique ring, Sue still slid it onto her right ring finger to see what it would look like. Strangely, once she had it on, the silver didn't appear as tarnished. She held up her hand, admiring the simplistic beauty of the piece.

"Keeping you would be wrong," she said to the jewelry. Her finger tingled where it touched her, and she flexed her hand, wondering if the band was a little too tight.

Leaving it on, she picked up her phone and searched for the hospital's number.

"*Put the phone down,*" a voice demanded loudly.

The sudden burst of sound caused Sue to jump in surprise. Realizing it was only an exuberant commercial for an ambulance-chasing law firm boasting million-dollar payouts, she laughed and resumed her search. Finding the hospital, she tapped the screen to call.

"*I said put the phone down!*" a woman's voice chided. "*Don't call until you know who to call.*"

Sue glanced at the television in annoyance as she lifted the phone to her ear. It was silent.

She checked the screen. The call hadn't started. She tapped the screen again and watched to make sure the call went through this time. As it began to ring, she held it to her ear with her shoulder.

Folding the check, she placed it with her

wedding ring and the jewelry box inside a zipper pocket in her purse for safekeeping.

"*Stop what you're doing,*" a car commercial demanded.

The phone stopped ringing and went silent.

"Hello?" She paused and listened. "Hello?"

Sue checked the phone. It had exited to the home screen.

"*For a limited time, escape in a brand-new sedan,*" a salesman dressed as a ninja offered. Technology might have changed, but car commercials were as stupid as ever. The word escape began echoing as the ninja posed, "*Es-cape. Es-cape. Es-cape.*"

Sue patted around the couch, looking for the remote. She finally found it trapped between two cushions. She muted the television and dropped the remote on the couch before reaching for her phone to try again. The screen flashed and went black.

"Great," she mumbled in annoyance, dropping the dead phone into her purse. At least walking to the cellular store would give her something to do in the morning.

Sue reached for her tea to take a drink. The cooling liquid passed her lips—and instantly set her mouth on fire. She spat bourbon at the television in surprise, opened her mouth wide, and breathed fast to try to calm the burning sensation.

Lifting her teacup, she sniffed the hard liquor inside it. "How in the...?"

Sue gathered the cup and plate and took them to the kitchen.

"What the hell is wrong with me?" She dumped the liquor down the sink. The taste of bourbon lingered in her mouth. She didn't remember pouring it.

The sound of television static came from the living room. The steady light from the lamp flickered off, replaced by the bright television light cast on the doorway.

A click sounded, and the channel changed. The light became softer. She slowly walked toward the doorway.

*"Enjoy our quaint coastal..."*

"Is someone here?" Sue called, really hoping she didn't get an answer. "Kathy?"

Hank's mother had a key to the house. The woman might have come over when Sue didn't answer the phone.

*"You've never experienced a place like Freewild Cove, North Carolina."*

The television blipped again, and a woman belted out a soulful song. *"Run away. Time is short."*

"Kathy, is that you in there channel flipping?" Sue's voice came out in a shaky whisper. She leaned to look past the doorway into the empty living room. The remote was on the couch where she'd left it.

The channel changed again, and an angry man covered with tattoos pressed his face to the bars of a jail cell and yelled, *"You better watch your fucking back. I won't be trapped forever, and when I get out—"*

"Hello?" Sue demanded. "This isn't funny."

A black-and-white movie replaced the jail scene. The Mid-Atlantic accent of a 1920s movie star boasted, *"I'm from North Carolina, and there's something you need to know about girls from North Carolina. We don't give up without a fight."*

Sue glanced around the empty room before slowly making her way toward the couch. She stood by the arm and stared at the changing screen.

*"Run away, run away, run, run, run!"* the woman sang desperately into her mic.

The channel changed to a closeup of a clown holding a knife next to his face. *"I'm coming for you."*

Sue took a deep breath. She believed in logical explanations, not the paranormal. Mrs. Dane at the store had joked that Mercury was in retrograde and that would make electronics malfunction. The cable provider had once issued some statement about radiation or sunspots or something messing with signals. That sounded like a reasonable, science-y explanation she could get behind.

Sue picked up the remote and hit the power button. The unit didn't respond. She walked closer to the television and hit the button repeatedly with her index finger.

*"You've never experienced a place like Freewild Cove..."*

Sue reached for the power cord and yanked the plug from the wall. The television turned off. She breathed a sigh of relief.

Without the television, darkness flooded the space. The drawn curtains blocked the view of the street. Sue blindly navigated the living room, letting her leg brush along the edge of the coffee table. She reached her hand out and walked until she felt the wall. Her fingers moved around a corner and down the hallway toward her bedroom.

Her hand met the door, and she skated her fingers to the doorknob.

Static sounded behind her, and her shadow flashed next to her. Sue flung around in surprise.

The television had turned on.

"I turned you off." Shaking, she forced herself toward the light. "I unplugged you."

She flipped the hall light switch as she passed it. The remote remained on the couch. Sue passed in front of the television.

A black-and-white closeup of a woman's face filled the screen, and the actress seemed to stare directly at Sue. She wore a sleek hat and dark lipstick indicative of film noir, as the serious male voice narrated, *"I could see the lady was frightened by the way she lingered in my doorway, even after I invited her in. I'd seen this kind of desperate look before. She was in danger, and she needed my help."*

Sue looked at the plug. It was in the wall.

*"You've never experienced a place like Freewild—"*

Sue pulled the cord and watched the plug come free of the wall before draping it over the edge of the television.

"I unplugged you. I'm looking at you, and you're unplugged. The television is unplugged." Sue took a deep breath.

Cedar and gun oil filled her nose. She hated that smell. Why wouldn't it go away?

"It's just phantosmia," she whispered, unable to

stop her hands from trembling. Sue walked with purpose down the hall. "I need to sleep."

*"Magic is real. I've seen it, Bev."*

Sue stopped halfway down the hall as a contemporary soundtrack played behind the woman's excited words. The mounting terror caused her eyes to fill with tears. She'd unplugged the television and hung the cord. She knew she had. She heard the small blip of channels changing as the voices continued.

*"Have you ever been to North Carolina?"* a man asked with a slight twang.

*"You've never experienced a place like Freewild Cove, North Carolina,"* the travel commercial insisted.

*"I escaped across the moors,"* a British lady sounded like she read from a book, *"away from the tyranny of my father's house."*

*"...run away, run, run..."*

Sue sprang into action. She ran into her bedroom and grabbed a suitcase from the closet. She didn't think as she threw things into the bag, scooping up armfuls of clothes and shoving them inside.

*"...a place like Freewild Cove, North Carolina."* The volume became louder.

Sue zipped the bag and dragged it behind her

down the hallway. The plug was in the wall, and the television kept flipping through channels. She snatched her purse from the coffee table.

"*Freewild Cove, North Carolina,*" the television practically screamed.

As she was backing away from the couch, she caught movement. The remote lifted on its own to hover in the air. The television screen paused on a beach scene, rewound a few frames, only to play.

"*Freewild Cove.*"

It did it again.

"*Freewild Cove.*"

And again.

"*Freewild Cove.*"

Sue ran for the door.

"*Freewild Cove.*"

It slammed shut behind her with unnatural force.

The evening had turned to dark, and she saw a hint of light playing through the seam in the curtains. She couldn't go back in. Head-injury-induced hallucinations or not, that shit was terrifying.

She stood on the front sidewalk and glanced up and down the quiet block, unsure what she was doing. It was late, and the only car she owned was spending its eternity in a junkyard. All she knew was she couldn't go back into the house.

The smell of cologne drifted past, bringing with it a chill.

Sue hurried down the sidewalk, keeping her head down and hoping none of her neighbors chose that moment to look outside.

# CHAPTER THREE

SUE TRIED NOT to look at the series of beach pictures that the bored teenager next to her kept flipping through on his phone. His parents were in the seats behind them. Every once in a while, his mother would try to hand him a water bottle and snacks. The kid would answer by shifting in the seat, slouching down as if to hide the bikini babe he'd found, and then sighing in annoyance. His leg encroached on Sue's space, but instead of saying anything, she leaned closer to the window.

The tinted windows kept the interstate lights from shining in her face as they traveled past the dark landscape. She'd been on the bus for—*gah, what was it, fifteen?*—hours, and as much as she hated being crammed next to two dozen strangers, she needed their nearness. Whatever weirdness had followed her through town until she'd ended up taking refuge at a bus station didn't seem to stir around the other passengers.

The screen of a tablet reflected in the window next to the seat in front of her. Though she couldn't hear the words, she saw the face of the clown with a knife. She knew it was impossible, but it felt like the clown smiled directly at her. She hugged her arms across her chest. The screen flashed to that of a couple in deep conversation at a restaurant. It didn't look like the same movie.

Sue turned her gaze to the back of the seat. The teenager suddenly jerked, hitting her shoulder with his elbow.

"Ow." Sue rubbed her arm.

"Sorry," the kid mumbled, but he continued playing a video game.

She pressed closer to the window to give him space. Her purse sat on the floor, squished between her feet. She thought of the check shoved in the zipper pocket of her purse, thankful she'd had the presence of mind to grab the bag.

Fear beat through her, tightening in her chest and flowing through her nervous limbs. She tried to convince herself that she'd hallucinated the remote hovering in the air, just like she hallucinated the smell of Hank's cologne.

Sue glanced at the teenager's phone just as he crashed the car he drove in the game. It flipped off the side of a cliff and exploded. She looked toward the window. The clown face was there, as he threatened with his knife. Tears gathered, and she closed her eyes.

*In. Out. In. Out.*

She had to calm herself, or she'd find herself screaming nonsense on a bus full of people.

"I can't wait to get to the beach," a woman said.

Sue had no idea where she was going. She had bought a ticket on the first bus leaving the station— anyplace to get away from the cloud of Hank's cologne following her down the sidewalk. She couldn't shake the feeling that she was doing something wrong, which was ridiculous. If she wanted to buy a bus ticket and travel all night, she should be able to do that.

Hank didn't like her traveling alone.

"Fuck Hank," she whispered. "I can if I want to."

"You want this? I'm done with it."

Sue opened her eyes. The woman in the seat ahead of her held a magazine toward her. Sue automatically lifted her hand to take it even though she didn't feel like reading. "Uh, thanks."

She put the magazine on her lap. A model's smiling face graced the cover next to the bold words, *"Know when to shut your mouth."*

One of the scented inserts that advertised cologne had slipped to the side. A nerve in her hand stung, and she looked at the ring she'd found in the hospital bag. In her flight from the house, she'd forgotten about it.

The teenager bumped her again, causing the magazine to slide on her lap. The scented insert slipped farther from the pages. With a shaking hand, Sue pulled it out. A glass of bourbon neat was printed on it, and the smell of gun oil and cedar wafted over her. The smell made her sick to her stomach.

"Cool. Can I have that?" the teenager asked.

Sue looked from the insert to the boy, not following his question. He gave a meaningful look at the cologne ad. She slowly handed it to him. The teen snatched it from her and instantly peeled it open to rub the scented paper on his neck. The stench of the cologne became unbearable.

"Do you know if we're stopping soon?" Sue asked.

The teen shrugged and went back to his game. "Probably never. This stupid trip..."

His words disappeared into a grumble as his attention disappeared into his game.

Sue rubbed her sore hand. Even though she hadn't wanted it, she opened the magazine to distract her mind from the overwhelming smell of her cologned neighbor.

She flipped to the center of the magazine to an article about a historic theater screening old movies. Sue almost ignored it but for an emblem carved in the front of the building. It looked similar to the band she wore. She turned the band on her finger and lifted it next to the picture. They were almost identical.

What could that mean?

"Warrick Theater," she read, mouthing the words quietly, "named for eccentric businesswoman Julia Warrick, who'd commissioned the building in the early nineteen-hundreds, represents a colorful chapter in North Carolina's history. A self-proclaimed medium, Julia wanted a place to hold séances. People would travel for hundreds of miles to have her contact their dead relatives."

The smell of the cologne tickled the back of her throat, and she gave a light cough. Sue tried to ignore it as she looked at a series of photos. Inside, the art deco theater appeared well maintained, if not a little outdated. She couldn't remember the last time she'd seen gold and burgundy sponge-painted walls.

Seeing a picture of a woman with dark hair standing behind a concession counter, Sue read, "Julia's granddaughter, Heather Harrison, is keeping the entertainment tradition alive and the theater doors open."

Sue started to pull the ring off her finger to get a better look at the design.

The bus lurched. A collective gasp of surprise sounded. Sue braced her hands to keep from flying out of her seat. The magazine slid off her lap and under the seat in front of her.

*Thud. Thump-thump-thump-thump. Clank.*

They bounced in their seats as the bus slowed.

"Oh, that can't be good," the teenager's mom exclaimed.

"Duh," the boy mumbled.

Sue leaned against the window, seeing the lights of a service station beckoning them as the bus turned off the interstate.

A staticky voice came over the intercom, "We're sorry for the interruption, folks. It looks like we're going to have to make an unscheduled stop. Feel free to stretch your legs and relax as we work out a solution and check back in twenty minutes."

The bus continued to bounce as it rolled into the service station parking lot.

She watched people stand up in anticipation of leaving the bus. Sue didn't want them to leave her alone. She didn't want to get off, either. There was a strange kind of safety in the lit cabin full of strangers, a comfort in knowing the bus rolled forward for endless miles, as if here, in this moment of perpetual movement onwards, nothing could catch her.

The passengers filed off the bus, giving her no choice but to grab her purse and follow. It had stopped on the far side of the parking lot, away from the front doors of a gas station boasting a connected fast food restaurant that served fried chicken and tacos.

She walked slowly as the others hurried past. As she went between a couple of gas pumps, a man said, "That didn't sound good at all. You guys all right?"

Sue stumbled to a stop and looked around. Kind brown eyes met hers. The directness of his gaze took her by surprise, and she didn't answer.

He gestured toward the bus. "Sounds like you guys had a bit of road trouble."

"Oh, ah..." Sue needlessly looked back at the

broken-down bus. "Yeah, engine, I think. Or tire, maybe? I don't know. There was a lot of thumping and clanking."

"I'm Jameson Lloyd." Jameson held his hand out to her and kept smiling, but she didn't trust his smile.

Hank smiled all the time too. People thought he was terrific.

"Sue." She ignored the offered hand. "Susan, Sue."

"Nice to meet you, Susan Sue." He pushed his dark hair away from his face with the back of his rejected hand.

He turned his attention to his car and pulled the nozzle from the red sedan's gas tank.

"Hey, Jameson, can I ask you something?" Sue stepped closer. "Where are we? What town? The driver didn't say when he kicked us off the bus while he figures out what's wrong with it."

"Freewild Cove," he answered. "We're about a half-mile from the beach. Not a bad place to get stranded. Though I live here, so I'm biased."

Freewild...?" She looked around. The nerve in her hand tingled, and she absently rubbed it. What were the odds that she'd see a commercial and then get blindly on a bus that broke down in the exact same town it advertised?

And the magazine article mentioning séances?

And the picture of the beach on the teenager's phone?

"Cove," he finished when the word got stuck in her throat. "Freewild Cove."

"Heather Harrison," she whispered, tugging at the ring. It didn't slide off her swollen finger.

"Oh, yeah, sure, I know Heather." Jameson continued to smile, the look friendly and unassuming. "She just moved into the Old Anderson House, right? I was happy to hear someone bought that old place to renovate it. It's a beautiful historic property."

"I don't know. I saw her name in an article I was reading on the bus." Sue glanced around the parking lot. "Warrick Theater."

"Sure, sure, I know it," Jameson said. "It's downtown. Another great historical building."

"I need..." Sue took a deep breath. Need sounded too desperate. "I want to see it."

"It won't be open this time of night," he said.

"Yeah, of course." She walked toward the gas station. "Thanks for the information."

"No problem," Jameson called after her. "Maybe I'll see you around if you decide to stay and check out the theater."

Before she answered, a loud clang came from the

bus. She turned to see smoke billowing from under the hood. The bus driver cursed and flung his arms in agitation before he began pulling the luggage from the baggage compartment. He tossed the bags unceremoniously next to the bus.

"Come on, Jerry, we need to find a hotel before all the rooms are taken," a woman from the bus said, pulling on her husband's arm. "There is no way they're going to be able to get a replacement out here tonight, and I'm not sleeping on the sidewalk while we wait for them to tell us as much. I told you we should have flown but you wanted to save a few bucks. I hope you're happy. You get what you pay for, Jerry."

Sue went back toward the bus to grab her suitcase, unsure what she should do next. This wasn't a planned trip. No one knew where she was or why. The only person she could think to call was Hank's mother, and she would come with a lecture about responsibility and a guilt trip.

The smell of Hank's cologne stirred around her. She needed to get out of there.

"That definitely can't be a good sign." Jameson appeared next to her. "Listen, there's a hotel a few blocks that way."

Sue watched him point but didn't take her eyes

off him. She hugged her purse against her. "I'm not looking for a date."

"What, oh, date? No." Jameson laughed. "I'm sorry, no, you're right. That sounded forward of me. I just meant there's a hotel close if you're going to be stuck here for the night. I can drop you there if you want. It's on my way."

"Thanks, but I'll figure it out." Sue walked faster, giving the man no choice but to end the conversation.

She told herself that not every man was Hank. Not every smile had something hiding behind it. Still, the easiness of Jameson's expression made her nervous. She couldn't help it. Nor could she help her response to it, and the feeling that at any moment, something solid would slam into her stomach as punishment for daring to talk to him.

The smell of gun oil and cedar drifted with her as she walked toward her luggage. Jameson's car drove past slowly as he made his way out of the gas station parking lot. Their eyes met, and she looked away first.

Her suitcase was on its side in a shallow puddle. She frowned as she lifted it from the ground. Muddy water dripped down the side.

"Folks, it looks like we're going to be here a while," the driver said. "If you'd like to wait in the restaurant, I'll let you know as soon as I hear something."

Sue glanced at the giant lettering on the window boasting fast food chicken and tacos. Through the window, she could see that already the booths were filling up with passengers.

Sue lifted her suitcase and began the long trek in the direction where Jameson had pointed.

"If you leave, we can't guarantee a refund," the driver called after her.

Sue lifted her hand to indicate she'd heard him and kept walking. She had no idea where she was going or if they'd have rooms available when she got there. The knowledge made her both nervous and excited, mostly nervous because she was in Freewild Cove due to a possessed television.

*In. Out. In. Out.*

She steadied her breath to match the rhythm of her pace. The sound of interstate traffic zoomed above the frontage road she traveled. The busyness contrasted with the lonely walk. If she didn't think about it, the suitcase wasn't too heavy. The streets created pockets of light on the ground between stretches of shadows. She quickened her steps when she went through the dark.

*In. Out. In. Out.*

As she walked around a curve, a hotel sign lit up the sky, boasting vacancies. She sighed in relief and hurried toward it. No one would know she was there. Sue had no choice but to keep moving forward. She could hide away in a room, surrounded by people but alone. One scream, and they'd come running.

*In. Out. In. Out.*

Sue went into the lobby. The woman behind the front desk reversed her coffee cup mid-drink as she smiled. "Welcome to Dicken's Inn. Do you have a reservation?"

"No, I'm sorry. I saw you had vacancies on the sign." Sue wasn't sure why she was apologizing for being a walk-in. She hated that about herself, always saying sorry even when it wasn't necessary. The word had always fallen out of her mouth like a preemptive strike against Hank's moods.

"That's quite all right. Is there just one?" The woman went to her computer and began typing.

"Yes. I'm alone." Sue glanced at the woman's name tag. "Agnes. That's a pretty name."

"Thank you, hon. Smoking or non?"

"Non." Could she ask for a room without television?

"I have a king- or queen-size bed." Agnes glanced

up and smiled. "Actually, it's late. I'm going to give you a suite for the regular room price."

"Oh, ah, thank you," Sue said in surprise. She reached into her purse and grabbed her license and credit card.

"License plate number?"

"No car. I was on a bus, and it broke down at the gas station down the road. I walked here." Sue glanced out the window, half expecting other passengers to show up.

"No worries." Agnes took her credit card, ran it through the reader, and then handed it back to her. "You're all set, Susan Jewel. Checkout is normally ten, but I'll write you in for a late check out so you can stay until noon. Breakfast is complimentary. It opens at six. Wi-fi password is right here." She circled the room number printed on the envelope holding the key card and then handed it to Sue. "You're in room 336. Elevators are down the hall to your left."

"Thank you." She started to turn, only to stop. "Any food delivery nearby?"

"Pizza. Numbers are in the binder in the room. Or, if you're desperate, there are cookies around the corner under the plastic dome."

Sue gave a small laugh. "Yeah, desperate."

The front desk phone began to ring.

"Help yourself, sweetie." Agnes waved Sue toward the cookies as she picked up the phone.

The chocolate chip cookies looked a little sad on their plate, but she grabbed a handful on her way to the elevator. A grinding, creaking noise sounded over her head as the elevator moved. She shoved a cookie into her mouth and chewed. The taste of hard liquor-filled her mouth and she coughed the cookie into her hand. She stared at the moist blob, going so far as to sniff it. It smelled like chocolate, but the aftertaste in her mouth was all smoky bar and cheap booze.

No. It was Hank's kisses. His mouth tasted like bourbon and cigarettes after he'd been out drinking with his buddies.

The elevator jerked to a stop, and the doors opened on the third floor. She trembled as she stepped into the hall, dragging her suitcase in one hand while clutching the cookie mash in her other. A maid cart was parked in the hall, and she grabbed a fresh towel to wipe the cookie off her hand before dropping it into the dirty laundry bag on the side.

Sue had to look at the key card envelope for her room number and instantly forgot it again as she moved her tongue around her mouth in a failed attempt to get rid of the taste. She looked yet again and whispered, "Three-three-six. Three-three-six."

In her over-concentration to find it, she almost walked past it. Shaking, she shoved the card into the key slot and then pressed the door open with her shoulder. Once inside, she released a breath she felt as if she'd been holding for hours.

Sue dropped her bags on the floor and threw the cookies in the bathroom trashcan. The suite was nothing special, looking like a billion other hotel suites just like it in the world—soft pastel walls and nondescript decor. She went to the television in the media cabinet and pulled its cord from the wall before turning the flat screen around to face the wooden back.

Her stomach growled with hunger, protesting the fact she'd thrown out the cookies. Sue grabbed a water bottle from the mini-fridge with its five dollar price tag. She closed her eyes and gulped as the blandness of water turned to the fire of burning liquor as it passed her lips. She tried to ignore it, filling her stomach as fast as she could.

Sue fell back on the bed, still in her travel clothes and not caring. Her hand tingled, and she pulled at the ring to get it off her finger. Everything had changed the second she'd put it on. None of what happened made sense.

Her lips still burned. She waited for the world to spin, but the water turned liquor did not carry alcoholic effects, and her mind remained unhappily aware.

# CHAPTER FOUR

Everything happened for a reason.

Sue wouldn't have believed that statement five months ago, but now, as she walked along a sidewalk to look up a woman whose name she'd read in a magazine article, she hoped it was true.

She had been scared into getting on the bus.

Someone thrust the article at her.

She met Jameson, who told her where to find Heather Harrison.

Every sign screamed Freewild Cove. So here she was in North Carolina, following a historical town map that had monstrously bad proportions drawn on it, looking for Old Anderson House.

*I'm officially a stalker,* she thought in dejection.

What else could she do?

Her hand shook as she held the tattered black box with the antique ring. It had taken soap and a lot of pulling to get it off her finger. Hunger and exhaustion tainted each step and made it hard to concentrate. Everything she put into her mouth tasted like liquor and ash. If she'd slept at all the night before, she wouldn't know it. She'd closed her eyes and tried, but her mind wouldn't shut off.

Moving vans passed her on the otherwise quiet road. Sue kept her gaze on the uneven sidewalk as to not make eye contact with the people inside. Tufts of grass pushed through the cracks, and she stepped around them.

Fear lingered in her, causing her heart to beat fast. Sue expected someone to jump out at her from each tree she passed. This was insanity. She knew it. She felt it. She still kept walking.

The wind picked up, bringing with it a chill. She caught the scent of cologne, a fleeting whiff as the breeze carried it past.

*In. Out. In. Out.*

All she could do was walk and breathe and pray Heather Harrison didn't think she was insane.

The faint sound of female laughter came from up the block. Sue quickened her pace. A woman stood looking toward where the moving vans had disappeared. She recognized Heather from her picture in the magazine.

Heather wore her long, dark hair pulled away from her face, and jeans with a flannel shirt. There was a natural beauty to her as if she didn't try too hard. Broken-down moving boxes were stacked by the driveway. It seemed fitting that the looming Victorian would have a local name, Old Anderson House. The half-painted siding contrasted old and new, what had been and the possibility of what could be.

When Heather didn't notice her and started to go inside, Sue said, "Excuse me?"

The woman turned to look at her; her expression caught between surprise and a smile. When she looked at Sue's face, her smile dropped some into concern. Sue could well imagine what impression her wild red hair and sunken, tired eyes would give.

"I know this is going to sound strange, but..." Sue edged closer. She forgot to plan out what she was going to say. How did you explain supernatural signs leading you to a person's front lawn? "I think I'm supposed to be here. I think I'm meant to talk to you. I keep receiving signs that all point to this house."

Well, crap. Honesty was one way to go about it. Probably not the *best* way, though.

"I'm sorry?" Heather asked, confused. Why wouldn't she be? Sue sounded like a lunatic.

"Heather?" Another woman asked from the doorway, her voice concerned. The woman looked as if she was helping Heather move but still somehow managed to look like she was a midlife model at a magazine shoot and not doing manual labor. Her wavy brown hair looked just messy enough to be staged. The color matched her eyes. "What is it?"

Sue's hands shook as she fumbled open the jewelry box and took out the ring. The box fell to the ground, and she held the ring between her shaking fingers to show Heather the engravings. Her hand vibrated when she touched the metal. At first, she thought the sensation was from the ring being too tight and pressing on a nerve, but now as it vibrated down her fingers, she knew that wasn't the case. "Does this mean anything to you? Because when I touch it, I feel like I have to be here."

Heather twisted a ring on her forefinger as she narrowed her eyes, looking at the jewelry Sue held.

A third woman appeared in the doorway. Unlike the well-put-together brunette, this woman tied her reddish-blonde hair into a messy bun with thin strands of hair escaping in frizzy protest around her head. She tucked her long bangs behind her ear as they moved from the doorway to join Heather on the lawn.

Sue picked up the box from the ground. "You think I'm nuts, don't you?" She placed the ring in the box and closed the lid, needing the vibrations emanating from the jewelry to stop. "I'm sorry for bothering you."

"No, wait." The model shared a look with the other two.

"Are you hungry?" the blonde offered, coming toward her.

Sue was too tired to step away as she swayed on her feet.

"We're just about to have dinner," the blonde continued.

"Yes, please come in and sit down," Heather added. "I think maybe this is where you're supposed to be."

Sue stiffened as the blonde hooked an arm around her shoulders.

"It's okay," the blonde whispered as she guided Sue inside. "We're here to help you."

The blonde stopped in the front room. Boxes created neat stacks against the wall, and a couch had been placed in the center of the room. Though of an old design, the home had been restored. Art canvases leaned against the light brown painted walls as if someone contemplated decorating choices.

Even with unpacked boxes and strewn furniture, the house felt like a home. An impression hummed in the air, the kind of gentle electricity that emitted a welcome to all that entered. The smell of roasting meat only added to the effect.

Sue's stomach growled in response.

"What's Julia up to now?" she heard the midlife model whisper.

"I don't know," Heather answered, "but it can't be a coincidence that she shows up today of all days when we are moving into our new home. Plus, she has one of Julia's rings."

Sue frowned. Julia Warrick? The woman who built the theater? She couldn't still be alive, could she? That Julia would be over a hundred years old by now.

"I guess there is only one way to find out," Heather took several steps into the room and stopped to study Sue.

The model shut the front door and stated, more to herself than anyone else, "Here we go again."

"I didn't steal it." Sue held out the ring box to Heather. "I want to return it."

"Oh, no." Heather held up her hands and

stepped back, refusing to take it. She turned her hand to show the ring on her forefinger. "I already got my Julia ring. I don't need a second."

The blonde dropped her arm from around her shoulders.

Sue tried to give it to the blonde, who shook her head in return.

"Don't look at me, either," the model said. "We all have our Julia adventures well in hand. That one belongs to you."

"I don't..." Sue touched her head. She wanted to collapse from exhaustion. She placed the jewelry box on top of the moving boxes. "I think I need to sit down for a second."

"Of course." The blonde led her through an archway into a dining room. She pulled out a chair.

"Where is everyone?" Heather asked the blonde.

"When I saw we had a visitor, I sent them out back with Jan," the blonde answered. "It felt like the thing to do."

Heather nodded. "Good call. No need to overwhelm."

Suddenly, a strong wind blew the front door open, slamming it hard. The ring box flew through the living room, slid over the floor, and tapped against Sue's foot.

"Maybe you should put it on," Heather said. "Trust me. There's no fighting it."

The model went to close the door. "Yeah, before Julia's magic wrecks our new house."

"Things might seem difficult now, but they always work out." The blonde lifted the box off the floor and pressed it into Sue's hand. "What's your name?"

"Susan, but they call me Sue," she said. "Sue Jewel."

"Nice to meet you, Sue. I'm Lorna Addams," the blonde said. "This is Heather Harrison, and that is Vivien Stone."

"Hi." Sue set the ring box on the table. "Please, I just want to return your property. It was sent home with me by accident."

"Sent home from where?" Lorna sat on the seat next to her, leaning a little too close.

Sue inched back in her chair to put distance between them. "I was in the hospital. It came home in my belongings. The hospital staff probably dropped it in my bag on accident."

"Where was that?"

"St. Louis," Sue answered.

"And you came all this way just to return it?" Lorna asked.

"It's not mine," Sue insisted. "I don't want it."

"Yeah," Vivien said with a small laugh. She walked around to the other side of the table to sit across from her. "It is now."

"I don't want it." Sue tried to stand, but her legs felt weak, and she fell back into her seat.

"Hospital," Lorna reached for Sue's hand, but Sue pulled away from her touch. "What happened?"

"Nothing," Sue dismissed. Why were they talking about this? Why was she even here? Now that she was sitting in Heather's dining room, she felt like an idiot. Who just jumps on a bus not knowing where they are going? Who thinks they see signs in television commercials and cell phones?

"People don't usually go to the hospital for nothing," Heather said.

"Just a car wreck." Sue rubbed her temples.

"I don't think I've ever heard anyone say *just* when it comes to a car wreck that lands them in the hospital." Vivien tapped her fingers on the table and studied her. Her voice softened. "You lost someone, didn't you?"

How did she know?

Sue didn't answer.

"You're overwhelmed," Vivien continued. "You don't understand what's happening to you."

They weren't questions.

"And why wouldn't you be?" Lorna again reached for her, finally capturing her hand. "You're so tired."

Sue didn't like the pity she saw on their faces.

"And hungry," Lorna stated, letting go of her and standing. "I hope you like pork roast with a green pepper jelly glaze, lemon and parmesan asparagus, cheesy mashed potatoes, and homemade dinner rolls. We're moving in, so I didn't have time to make something elaborate for dessert, but there is chocolate cake."

"My something-not-elaborate is me picking up tacos from a food truck," Heather said. "Lorna's not-elaborate is something that only took her an hour to cook from scratch."

"It's why she's our roommate," Vivien said.

"I heard that," Lorna called from the other room.

"There are other reasons," Vivien loudly amended.

"Yeah, your baking," Heather added.

To Sue, Vivien said, "You have got to try her cinnamon rolls. I know that after forty, I'm supposed to watch what I eat because I can't lose weight as fast, but, baby, buy me a forklift because I cannot say no to her cinnamon rolls."

Lorna poked her head through the doorway. "I can do that. You want regular or chocolate chip cinnamon buns? I have the stuff to make both."

"Oh, no, wait, stop, you don't have to do that," Vivien droned in a flat tone, clearly not meaning it. Then more enthusiastically, she added, "Chocolate chip."

"Unless you prefer regular?" Heather said to Sue.

"No, I..." Sue shook her head. They acted like she was going to stay there awhile. The thought of putting anything in her mouth made her gag. "None for me."

"You have to eat something." Lorna came more fully into the room and placed her hands on her hips.

"I..." Sue looked at the ring box on the table but didn't touch it. "I can't."

"Are you allergic?" Heather asked. "Because we can accommodate allergies, right Lorna?"

"Of course," Lorna said.

Sue thought about lying, but these women were being nice to her. They invited her into their home, and even though they were a little strange, she had no reason to be mean to them.

Sue shook her head. "No."

"Don't like pork?" Vivien asked.

"No, it's not that, it's..." Sue continued to stare at the ring box. "Nothing tastes right. I think my mouth is cursed." She frowned, tucking her chin a little as she drew her eyes to the floor. "And my nose."

"Cursed?" Heather took the seat Lorna had previously occupied.

"It's just a saying," Sue tried to dismiss.

"My mouth is cursed is not a saying. You can't judge a book by its cover is a saying," Vivien said. "The grass is always greener on the other side is a saying."

"Technically, I think those are clichés," Heather said, "but you made your point."

Vivien sighed and closed her eyes. She absently twirled the antique ring on her finger. "Everything you eat tastes like... like something else, something that makes you gag."

"How...?" Sue used the last of her strength to stand and step away from Heather. The second she was upright, she regretted it.

"We believe you," Heather said. "Whatever you tell us is happening, we will believe you."

"Dinner is almost ready," Lorna yelled from the kitchen. "I just need a few more minutes."

They ignored her.

"There is a smell too," Vivien continued. "A phantom smell that follows you?"

"You can't know..." Sue shook her head. It was too difficult to concentrate. "What did you do to me? That ring—"

"Oh, hey, no," Heather said. "Julia's rings aren't cursed. It came to you to be a guide because you need our help."

"Help with—?" Before Sue could finish the sentence, the smell of Hank's cologne surrounded her.

"What the hell is that smell?" Vivien pinched her nose and turned toward the kitchen doorway. "Lorna, is someone in there smoking fifty cigarettes?"

Sue coughed, covering her mouth even as she fell to her knees. The smell choked her, and it became hard to breathe. The air rasped from her lungs.

"Do you feel that?" Heather asked as she dropped to her knees beside Sue.

"It's freezing," Vivien said. "What do you see?"

"Nothing." Heather took hold of Sue's arms. "She's cold."

"Lorna," Vivien yelled. "We need you!"

Sue fell onto her side. Heather tried to catch her even as she eased her on the floor. The woman stroked back her hair from her face.

"I brought dinner rolls," Lorna said. "The food just came out of the oven, but I thought she could start on these. Where—*Omigod, what happened?*"

"She needs your help," Heather said. "Transfer whatever she has into me."

"And me," Vivien said. "We'll share it."

"We'll *all* share it," Lorna corrected. "Try to make her comfortable."

"I can..." Sue tried to sit up.

"Lie down," Heather ordered.

Sue moaned. Her head hurt, and she just wanted the darkness to take her.

When she opened her eyes, she saw the women leaning over her. She frowned and weakly swatted her hand to get them away. They ignored her.

"Let her help," Heather urged. "Lorna's a healer."

"I don't need reiki or whatever you call it," Sue protested, though the words sounded more like a mumble even to her own ears. The last thing she wanted was someone touching her, even if they claimed it was for therapeutic purposes. She was only vaguely aware that she was lying on the dining room floor in a stranger's home.

"Stop fussing and let us help you." Lorna touched Sue's forehead and then reached for

Heather's hand. Lorna closed her eyes. Sue felt her skin tingle where the woman made contact with her.

After a few seconds, Heather covered her mouth and yawned. "I don't know if I'm more tired or hungry."

"Give me the hunger pains," Vivien said. "I don't mind having seconds."

Lorna let go of Heather and grabbed Vivien, then placed her hand on Sue's stomach. Sue couldn't keep her eyes open. As the pain started to leave her, exhaustion set in.

Vivien grabbed her side. "Oh, fuck, that's not hunger pains."

Lorna instantly drew her hands away from Sue and Vivien. "What happened?"

Vivien lifted her shirt to show a bruise forming on her side. "I feel like someone just kicked the shit out of me."

Sue felt someone tugging on her shirt. Lorna said, "I don't see a bruise."

"That's because you gave it to me," Vivien stated.

"Here, let me hold it," Lorna answered.

"Don't touch me," Vivien said. "I'll be fine. It just took me by surprise."

"Is she," Heather's voice moved closer as she spoke, "sleeping?"

Sue was awake, barely, but made no effort to answer them. She didn't have anything left in her.

"Find the guys," Heather ordered. "Have one of them carry her upstairs. I'll go make sure there are sheets on my bed."

"I'll just sit right here," Vivien said. "Maybe bring me a painkiller when you're done? Or a bottle of wine. I don't care which. I have the strangest urge to be numb."

Sue tried to keep listening, but she couldn't move. She didn't know what kind of magic spell Lorna had worked with her hands, but Sue wasn't about to question it. For whatever reason, right now, here on the dining room floor of a stranger's house, she felt safe. With the pain gone and the hunger eased, she decided to let the darkness claim her.

# CHAPTER FIVE

THE SMELL of cinnamon rolls lured Sue from a deep sleep. It had to be a dream of the childhood she never experienced. Her mother drank. Her father left. Breakfast was a handful of cereal because they never had milk in the fridge. All her life, if she wanted cinnamon rolls, she had to make them herself.

Maybe this was another side effect of her head injury, another... what was it called?

She opened her eyes, not recognizing the bedroom. The blue-grey walls looked pristine, and a hint of fresh paint lingered behind the cinnamon rolls.

*Phantom? No. That's not it.*

Sue sat up on the king-sized bed. The dark blue quilt looked new, but someone had scuffed the white

MICHELLE M. PILLOW

paint on the antique bed frame to make it appear old. Stacks of moving boxes waited along a wall. She pulled the quilt off her legs and hurried to a window to look out at the lawn. She was on the second story of Old Anderson House.

The smell lingered. Didn't people smell cinnamon rolls before they had a stroke? Or during? She was sure she'd heard that somewhere.

*Phantasm? No. Shit, what is it called?*

Why couldn't she remember?

Sue's brain felt foggy, as if she'd slept too long and had a hard time coming out of the dream and into reality. She didn't belong here. She couldn't go home.

Sue took a deep breath, thankful for the reprieve from gun oil and cedar.

*What is it—?*

"Good, you're awake."

"Phantosmia," Sue said, as she turned in surprise at the sound.

Heather smiled at her. "Excuse me?"

"Olfactory hallucination," Sue tried to explain. "I was trying to remember... It doesn't matter. Ignore me."

"You think you're hallucinating?" Heather's

smile faded, and she came into the room, looking around. After a few seconds, she relaxed.

"I smell cinnamon rolls." Sue stayed by the window, very aware of how strange this situation continued to be.

"Oh, that is not a hallucination. That heavenly smell is Lorna baking." Heather gestured for Sue to come with her. "Why don't you come down and eat? You have to be starving."

"I should get back to my hotel." Sue looked for a clock but couldn't find one. "I need to ask them to let me stay longer. My luggage... How long have I been here?"

"Dicken's Inn, right?" Heather again motioned that she should follow her.

"How...?" Sue frowned.

"Vivien made a few calls." Heather chuckled. "Seriously, this is a small town. Lodging options are limited. Don't worry. It's all been taken care of. I sent Martin—he's my manfriend—to go pick up your luggage."

"I can pay for my room. I don't need help." Sue refused to leave the window. She crossed her arms over her chest. She wasn't a charity case.

"I don't mean to be rude, but, sweetie, look at your hand." Heather leaned against the doorframe.

Sue glanced at her hand and found the ring was back on her finger. She began to shake.

"It's not an accident that you're here." Heather moved slowly closer and held out her hands. "I don't know what or why, but I do know that Julia's rings are never wrong. They go to those who need them. Like me."

Sue didn't take the offered hands.

"Like Vivien. Like Lorna. We all needed something, and together we found the answer." Heather took Sue's hands in hers. "And now we're going to help you."

At the contact, the shaking stopped. Sue felt a strange sensation filling her as if it flowed from Heather's hands into her. There was an eagerness to help, but beneath that was the echo of pain.

"What...?" Sue couldn't understand what was happening. She felt a dull sadness, but it wasn't her own. It came from Heather like an emotional beacon.

"You're so scared," Heather whispered. A tear slipped down her cheek. "Oh, I feel it, the fear in you. You're terrified all the time."

Sue snatched her hands back. "No."

Heather wiped her tear away. "You're scared of saying the wrong thing."

"No," Sue denied, even though she knew it was a lie.

"Of displeasing...who?" Heather again tried to touch her, and Sue sidestepped her.

"I have no one, so there is no one to displease," Sue said. "My mother passed years ago. My father disappeared when I was a kid. My husband..."

Sue shook her head.

"The car accident you were talking about?" Heather asked.

"He died," Sue said.

"So—"

"I don't want to talk about it." Sue left the room, not knowing where she was going. Seeing stairs, she hurried down them to a landing that split into two directions. She started left and stopped as the smell of cinnamon rolls became stronger. She went right and found herself in the living room by the front door.

A knock sounded seconds before the door opened. "Delivery!" A man wearing brown work pants and a t-shirt entered carrying her luggage. He'd tucked his dark hair under a black bandana. Seeing Sue, he smiled. "You must be Sue. I'm Martin."

Sue took a step back. He had a kind smile but exuded physical strength. Her eyes inadvertently went to his hands on the bag. They were a workman's hands, rough and scarred and strong.

"I hope I got everything," he said.

"Thank you, hon," Heather answered for her, thumping down the stairs. She patted Sue on the shoulder lightly as she passed and went to Martin. She gave him a quick kiss. "Would you mind putting them in my room for her?"

"No," Sue said, more confident now that she wasn't alone with Martin. "I can't stay."

"You can't leave." Vivien joined them from the dining room.

"Sorry to drop and run, but I have to pick up January from school," Martin said. "They just called."

Heather frowned. "This early?"

"Well, ah..." Martin glanced at Sue.

"Julia sent her to us," Vivien said. "Sue's cool."

"Someone confronted her about talking to an empty desk," Martin said. "I guess she was calling it the name of some classmate who died a few years ago before we moved here. Some of the kids took offense and threw a book at Jan. She's fine, just a little bruised. They thought it best I pick her up."

"Bring her here," Heather said. "We'll talk to her."

"I was hoping you'd say that." Martin gave Heather another kiss before rushing out the door.

"Poor Jan," Heather said.

"Poor Martin," Vivien added. "None of this can be easy for him."

"Is Jan a troublemaker?" Sue asked.

"No, she's just having a little trouble telling the difference between ghosts and livies," Vivien said.

"Livies?" Sue frowned.

"Alive people," Vivien said.

Sue thought maybe she was supposed to laugh, but their expressions didn't change. "Ghosts?"

"You know you have one stuck to you, right? That is why you came to us," Vivien stated.

Sue quickly looked around. Fear prickled the back of her neck. "No. That's not real. The accident. I have a head injury. The doctor said I..."

"Viv, come on, a little tact," Heather scolded.

"Trust me. Blunt is better, like pulling off the supernatural bandage really fast. Get the sting over with so we can get down to business." Vivien arched a brow toward Sue. When Sue didn't answer, Vivien lifted her shirt to show a bruise on her side. "Look familiar?"

Sue looked at the ring on her hand. Her finger tingled. "Hank?"

Had Hank done something to Vivien? How was that possible? She had been at his funeral. They buried him. If ghosts were real and not a hallucination caused by the accident, why didn't more people know about them? Scientists would have said something. News of sightings would have erupted all over the internet—not just stupid light reflected dust particles people tried to call spirit orbs.

"Hank? Was that your husband?" Heather asked.

Sue nodded. "I smell him sometimes, his cologne, for no reason. I even replaced my pillows, but it's like he's coming into the room and laying down next to me. And then I started tasting him."

"Tasting him?" Vivien repeated. "You mentioned your mouth being cursed."

Lorna appeared quietly next to Vivien in the doorway, listening.

"I taste what he used to taste like after he'd been drinking and smoking, which had been almost every night." Sue took a deep breath. Why was she telling them this? "Everything I put into my mouth, whether it's water, a sandwich, a cookie, it tastes wrong and burns when I swallow."

Vivien dropped her shirt to cover the bruise.

"Did I... bump you when I fell?" Sue had been so

tired when she arrived. She remembered falling and them discussing moving her to a bedroom.

"Lorna transferred the injury from you to me," Vivien said.

Sue remembered Lorna touching her when she was on the floor. Relief had come over her at contact. Her aches had lessened, and the hunger pangs had gone away.

"I'm a healer," Lorna explained. "Really that just means I can transfer illness from person to person. I know it sounds strange. Honestly, I'm getting used to it myself, but when I was trying to help you yesterday, that bruise moved from your side to Vivien's."

"I didn't have a bruise yesterday." Sue touched her side.

"Uh, yes, you did." Vivien gestured at her waist. "How else did I get this?"

"The last time I had a bruise-like that was months ago. It took a while to fade after the accident, but..." Sue shook her head. Was she having this conversation? Her side still ached sometimes, a residual pain that echoed in her memory, but the bruise had been long gone. "Is this some kind of—*I don't know*—a bad reality television show? Tease the new widow? Scare the stranger?"

"I know it's a lot to accept," Lorna said. "It was

for me. I can promise you, though, that this isn't some kind of sick prank. When I summoned my husband back from the dead, I didn't know what I was doing. I was so angry with him. I needed to give him a piece of my mind."

"Did he hurt you?" Sue hugged her arms to her waist in a protective gesture.

Lorna nodded. "After he died, I found out Glenn had another wife. I was his second."

"She was a piece of trashy work, too," Vivien muttered. At Lorna's glance, Vivien shrugged. "What? She was."

"His first wife was legally entitled to inherit everything, and my kids and I were left with practically nothing." Lorna had a sweetness to her, a soft-spoken natural goodness that was easy to see in everything she did. "The only good thing was that the kid's college tuition was all taken care of, so they at least got to keep that much. I couldn't take all the gossip about it, so I decided to move here to take a job at Heather's theater. That's when I found Julia's ring, or rather when it found me."

"Lorna is too nice to say it, but her ex was a real asshat, emphasis on the asshole," Vivien stated. "We sent Glenn's spectral ass packing."

"The point is, thanks to Julia's help, I was able to get closure," Lorna corrected.

"And she started dating Mr. William Warrick." Vivien grinned.

"Warrick?" Sue glanced at Heather.

"Yep, my brother." Heather sat on the arm of the couch and crossed her arms over her chest. "Though I'm not sure that had anything to do with the ring."

"Thanks to the rings, Vivien was able to say goodbye to her first husband, Sam. We found a message in a bottle from him buried at the beach," Lorna continued. "And Heather was able to say goodbye to someone as well."

Sue waited for them to elaborate on Heather, but they didn't. They stared at her expectantly. She refused to speak.

"We can help you," Lorna said at length. "There is a way we can bring the dead to us to talk."

Were they insane? She didn't want to call Hank back from the dead for a conversation. Summoning a demon from the depths of hell sounded like more fun. A devil would probably get less pleasure out of kicking the shit out of her too. "I don't want to say goodbye to anyone. I don't want to confront anyone. I just want to be left alone. I want the hallucinations to stop."

"Sometimes confronting them is the only way to get them to leave you alone. Sometimes you just have to say, 'I know you're there. You're dead. Leave me alone.' And sometimes it..." Vivien rubbed her temple and closed her eyes tight. She made a strange noise in the back of her throat. Then, almost dramatically, she whispered, "Oh my god, please tell me that it wasn't as bad as all that."

"What?" Heather rushed to Vivien. "What are you sensing?"

Vivien's demeanor had changed. The feistiness of her personality left her. When she opened her eyes, they were moist. She slowly shook her head. "Tell me he didn't do that to you. Not with a bottle."

Sue stared at the woman, horrified. There was no way Vivien could know any of what happened to her. No one knew.

Vivien opened her mouth and touched her lips.

"What?" Heather asked.

"We have to protect her," Vivien stated. "This isn't a normal haunting. It's not like Sam or Glenn. Sam was confused. Glenn was just an ass. This guy—"

"Don't," Sue begged, not wanting anyone to know. She'd kept the secret for so long. She took a step toward the front door and contemplated running out of the house.

Lorna and Heather turned to look at her, stopping her progress.

"Whatever happened, it's not your fault," Lorna said.

"Who told you about that?" Sue stared at Vivien. Tears brimmed her eyes. No one was supposed to know. The secret was to have died with Hank.

"You know how Lorna put her hands on you and healed you?" Heather approached her slowly. "Vivien has the ability to understand things about people, things they don't say out loud."

"Ghosts, talking to dead people, magical healing, mind reading." Sue frowned. "What are you? Witches?"

"No," Lorna said. "Well, kind of. Maybe. I'm a healer, and I'm good at locating lost objects. It's a new gift. I mean, I've always had caretaking tendencies with my family, but Julia's ring amplified it for me."

"I'm clairsentient," Vivien again rubbed her temple.

Sue inched away from the woman, not wanting her to pick up anything else from her past.

"I feel what other people are feeling and understand why they might be feeling that way," Vivien continued, "but also claircognizant because I know if things are real or not without always being able to explain how I know. My ancestors worked for carnivals as fortune-tellers and doing tarot card readings. I've never tried to divine the future. That seems like a tricky business."

"And you?" Sue asked Heather.

"I'm a medium," Heather stated. "I see and talk to ghosts. My grandmother, Julia, was the same way. It's a family trait."

Sue looked around the room. "Do you see them now?"

"No." Heather shook her head. "But this morning, there was one standing on our lawn in a bathrobe waving at something that wasn't there. He was completely unaware of me. Sometimes they're like that, a ghost trapped in some memory."

"And other times?" Sue wasn't sure if she should believe what they were saying. Trusting people wasn't exactly in her skill set.

"Other times they're more aware and vocal," Heather said. "And, then, there are a few who have to be forced to show themselves. They're usually the, uh—"

"Dangerous," Vivien inserted.

"—serious problems," Heather continued more diplomatically, "the ones who don't want to be seen because they have certain motivations driving them."

Sue watched them closely. What she had experienced, all the things that led her to this place, warred with reason. Logic told her that ghosts were not real. Magical healing powers were not real. Cursed rings were not real.

And yet, here she was. With each passing second, it became harder to deny what she was experiencing.

Sue didn't want this to be real. She wanted nothing more than to fade into a quiet and simple life.

"Cinnamon rolls," Lorna announced, waving them toward the dining room. "No more scary talk on an empty stomach."

Sue glanced at her luggage and then at the door.

"Don't even try it," Heather whispered. "Lorna will hunt you down and make you eat something. She looks sweet but trust me, that woman can mom you with the best of them."

Usually, having people stare at every bite of food she took would have been torture. Today, Sue didn't care. Food tasted like food, and she stuffed every morsel she could into her mouth out of fear that at any second it would turn to hard liquor and ash.

"Another?" Lorna asked, even as she placed a third cinnamon roll in front of Sue.

The haze over her thoughts began to clear as the sugar entered her system, taking with it the constant ache in her head.

"Coffee?" Lorna asked.

Sue nodded, taking a big bite.

"Maybe you should make another pan," Heather suggested.

Sue covered her mouth and mumbled, "I'm sorry. If I'm eating too—"

"She's teasing," Vivien said. "You eat as much as you want."

Sue had a hard time meeting Vivien's eyes. She could feel the pity in her gaze.

Lorna appeared with the coffee pot and refilled Sue's mug.

"Thank you." Sue set the half-eaten roll on the plate. "Would it be possible to get a ride back to the hotel? I should check back in."

"Nonsense," Lorna said. "You should stay here."

Sue shook her head, uncomfortable with the idea. "You just moved in. You're not even unpacked."

"We'll make room." Heather began to nod at the others for their agreement.

"I'll give you a ride wherever you want to go," Vivien contradicted.

"Viv." Lorna frowned. "She should stay here with us."

"She's clearly uncomfortable staying with strangers. Can you blame her?" Vivien stared at her again as if she was reading Sue's innermost thoughts. "She is magically terrorized to get here, confused and alone. We rip off those supernatural bandages, drop a few hey-guess-what-you're-one-of-us-now truth bombs, and then expect her to want to move in and join the séance party?

Sue shivered. Yes, that was exactly what she had been thinking—more or less.

"Not move in," Heather corrected. "Stay until we can figure this out, as our guest. That way, we can help keep an eye on things."

*I don't need a babysitter,* Sue thought.

"It's not like she needs us to babysit her," Vivien said. "Maybe we take her to the theater?"

*Stop doing that!* Sue tried not to scowl.

Vivien glanced at her but said nothing.

*Did you hear that? Look at me if you can hear this,* Sue thought.

Vivien didn't look.

Lorna took a deep breath. "The theater isn't a bad idea."

"Thank you for the offer, but I'm not really in the mood for a movie," Sue said.

"There's an unoccupied apartment above the theater lobby," Vivien explained.

"We have the new security system," Lorna added, directing her comment toward Heather. "If she pushes the panic button, we can be there in minutes."

"I can call Troy and have him set up a live feed from the concessions area today," Vivien said. "Wouldn't take much, and we could keep an eye out that way too."

"Are you talking about Warrick Theater?" Sue thought of the magazine pictures.

"Yes. I inherited the building. The upstairs studio apartment is completely furnished. Lorna was there not too long ago, so all it might need is a light dusting if that. You'll have to get groceries," Heather said. "You can stay as long as you want. No charge."

"I can pay," Sue said.

"No need," Heather answered. "Doesn't cost me anything to have you there."

"It's cozy," Vivien added. "Right downtown. Great Chinese restaurant across the street. An amazing coffee shop down the block."

"No television, though," Heather warned.

"I don't really like television," Sue said. It might have been a recent aversion, but it was still true.

"Scheduled groups come in and out during the day, and we sometimes show movies in the evenings," Lorna said. "I'm the manager, so I'll be there almost every day, but you'll have privacy when you want it."

Sue started to shake her head to turn down the offer. The ring sent a vibration down her hand. She found herself saying, "All right. Thank you."

"I'll find the extra keys." Heather pushed up from the table and walked out of the room. Her footsteps sounded running up the stairs.

"I'll go by the grocery store before work and bring you some supplies. Any requests?" Lorna picked up some of the dirty dishes from the table, leaving Sue's plate and mug so she could finish.

"You don't need to trouble yourself," Sue denied.

"No trouble." Lorna went into the kitchen.

"Pick up some wine for her, too," Vivien yelled. "A nice, strong red. She's out."

"Her or you?" Lorna called from the other room.

Vivien laughed. "Me!"

Lorna poked her head around the corner and asked Sue, "Do you drink wine?"

Sue nodded.

Lorna smiled and disappeared back into the kitchen.

"You're not used to people helping you, are you?" Vivien followed Lorna into the kitchen and came back seconds later with her purse. "I don't blame you for being distrustful after what you've been through, but we are here to help. No strings attached." She came to where Sue sat at the table and touched her shoulder. "I promise you will get through this. Whatever it is, you will get through it."

Sue nodded, unable to speak. As much as trusting anyone scared her, she felt their concern— open, unwavering, freely offered. When Vivien touched her, she imagined she knew the woman more than she should. She had a kind heart beneath her naturally sassy attitude. She understood loss and had loved deeply in her life.

Sue looked at Vivien's hand. "What's happening to me?"

"I've never been accused of being overly subtle,

and, honestly, I'm too old to start trying it now," Vivien said. "So I'm just going to lay it all out there."

"What?" Sue's shoulder tingled with awareness. It wasn't attraction, but an understanding, a familiarity that she'd never felt with another person.

Friendship? Could it be that?

"There is a magic in this world that most never recognize or name, but we all seek. It connects us as humans—we suffer, we hurt, we feel loss, we endure, we need, we love, we yearn, we cope, and we have secrets we want to share with others. Call it the human condition. Say it's because we're social creatures who instinctively reach out to bond with others." When Sue started to question, Vivien shook her head to stop her and continued, "That is what you're feeling between us now. The rings amplify our connection. You can feel me if you try, and you'll recognize that my intentions are honest, just as I can feel your fear. I don't know how to explain what you're feeling other than to say it's like you're that young girl in the horror movie hiding from the slasher under a bed as she watches his feet move around her room. You have your hand over your mouth, trying not to make a sound, too terrified to try to run. It's like you know it's only a matter of time before he catches you, but you keep hoping someone will make it go away. You've been stuck under that bed, watching those feet, for a very long time."

That was probably the aptest description of her feelings that anyone had ever guessed.

"Don't tell." Sue's voice shook as she glanced at the doorways to indicate Heather and Lorna.

"You know it's not your fault, don't you?" Vivien withdrew her hand.

Sue reached for her shoulder, where the sensation of the touch lingered. "Please, I don't want people knowing. I—" Her voice cracked.

*I don't want anyone to know.*

The shame she felt was unbearable.

"I won't tell because you ask me not to," Vivien assured her, "but I hope that one day you do. Don't let this bury you. Whatever he did to you, you did not deserve. You have nothing to be ashamed about."

"How...?" Sue took a deep breath. "How much do you know?"

"Got them!" Heather returned, holding the keys. "Ready? I texted Martin. He'll bring Jan by the theater to meet us."

Sue hated herself for being so relieved that Vivien hadn't answered her question. If she didn't have the answer, she could pretend the woman didn't know how bad it had been.

"Come on, Sue. We'll take you to the theater and get you settled." Vivien followed Heather.

Sue stood alone in the dining room. She reached for her coffee cup and took a sip. The liquid burned its way down her throat, and the faint smell of cologne filled the air. Her hand shook, and she slowly set the mug back on the table.

"Hank?" she whispered. "If that is you, I need you to go. You're not alive anymore."

There was more she wanted to say, but fear kept her from yelling at him. He'd always hated backtalk.

"I'm sure there is a giant party waiting for you on the other side," Sue kept her voice quiet, feeling a little foolish for talking to the air. "Fully stocked bar that never runs dry."

The smell lessened, and the air felt a little lighter.

Sue let loose a deep breath as she looked around the dining room. Had that worked? Could it really be so simple?

Vivien came to the doorway. "Sue? Everything all right?"

Sue nodded and hurried to leave. "Yeah, coming."

# CHAPTER SIX

"WARRICK THEATER," Sue read on the plaque affixed to the outside of the building. A small tremor worked over her as she saw Julia's name. The three friends had kept referring to the jewelry as Julia's rings. Seeing the woman's name on a bronze plaque along with a story of how she commissioned the building over a hundred years ago drove home just how much Heather, Lorna, and Vivien believed in their ghosts and magic.

"She was quite the lady, huh?" Vivien said, joining Sue by the plaque. She lightly ran her hand along the words, paraphrasing, "Suspected witch and part of the Spiritualist movement, Julia held séances in this theater to talk to the dead. People would travel hundreds of miles to come to her shows."

"Was Heather close to her?" Sue asked.

"Yes, very," Vivien said.

"Julia taught her how to be a medium?" Sue glanced down the sidewalk to where Heather paced while talking on the phone.

"No one had to teach Heather to see things. That happened whether she wanted it to or not. Julia taught her to understand it." Vivien also glanced at Heather before looking around the downtown area. "She helped me too. Mainly, she helped me realize I wasn't a freak for feeling the things I feel or sensing the things I sense about people. She taught me to trust myself."

Sue wished she could trust herself. She had once, but she hardly remembered the feeling. Hank had beaten it out of her. When she tried to hold on to her independence, he'd hit her harder. When she tried to leave, he'd come at her with flowers and an apology, and when that didn't work, he'd broken her arm.

"It's going to be all right," Vivien said.

Sue nodded, not answering. She had to stop thinking about Hank around this woman. Pointing at the plaque, she said, "Do you still do séance shows here?"

"No. This was back in the early 1900s. Freewild Cove likes its quirky past, but if we were to try to hold public séances, they'd probably riot and burn the building down. Trust me, having grown up here as that weirdo kid in class, I've seen firsthand how intolerant good folk can be when it comes to someone who isn't like they are."

"That's not special to Freewild Cove. People everywhere don't want to hear when things aren't like they think they are." Sue went to a window and cupped her hands around her eyes to look inside. She watched the shadows for movements.

"Don't worry." Vivien patted her shoulder but didn't let the contact linger. It sent tiny jolts of Vivien's emotions through Sue, so she detected Vivien's concern. "Julia always sent the spirits back when she was done talking to them."

"I wasn't worried," Sue lied. In truth, it freaked her out a little, like going into a reportedly haunted house.

Vivien lowered her voice as if telling a secret. "What the plaque doesn't say is that Julia Warrick made her money to pay for this building and several other properties in town by bootlegging moonshine and growing marijuana during Prohibition. She was quite the gangster."

"Is that true?" Sue asked.

Vivien nodded. "Heather and William inherited

a lot of the properties. They both went into construction. Heather rehabs old houses and turns them into rentals. William is more on the construction site and runs a crew, though he does flip houses."

"And you? What do you do?" Sue asked.

"Not much of anything." Vivien laughed, only to add, "I own several fast food restaurants."

The smell of sea air stirred along the sidewalk of downtown Freewild Cove. The buildings along the block looked as old as the theater. Cars filled the opposite side of the street, and a hefty amount of foot traffic went into the Chinese restaurant.

"Two words. Crab Rangoon." Vivien pointed at the restaurant. She moved her finger to indicate down the block. "That way, turn right at the end of the block, and you'll find a bookstore and coffee shop. Left will get you to an organic grocery food store. Pricey and small, but they have a great produce section. However, if Verna tries to get you to taste her homemade fruit cake ice cream, say no. It's chunky and not in a good way."

"No to chunky ice cream," Sue repeated with a nod. "Sounds like solid advice."

Several cars drove past, slowing as they neared the theater. The people in them openly stared at Sue and Vivien. Sue turned her back on them and pretended to look at the poster for an Elvis imperson- ator concert hanging in the glass case close to the theater's front door.

"It must be nice living so close to the beach," Sue said.

"It is. I think we take it for granted sometimes." Vivien leaned against the building and glanced to where Heather paced the sidewalk as she talked on her phone.

"Please don't touch the water main. I'll send one of my guys out to check the pipes—no, no, don't do that," Heather stated firmly. "I understand that your boyfriend has a special tool, but..."

Heather turned, and her voice became too hard to hear. She braced the phone on her shoulder, pulled a small notepad from her back pocket, and began writing on it.

"Her renters are always up to something," Vivien muttered. "She's too lenient with them."

"How so?"

"She probably won't make them foot the entire repair bill, even though it's their fault and what they did went against their lease," Vivien said. "She never charges as much as she should. On some of the prop- erties, she barely breaks even."

"I have money," Sue insisted, feeling guilty. "I don't mind paying for—"

"Okay, done!" Heather strode toward them, shoving her notepad and phone in her back pocket, only to reach into her front pocket to produce a set of keys.

"I didn't mean you," Vivien dismissed the concern. To Heather, she asked, "What was it this time?"

"Marianne has a new boyfriend. He tried to install a jacuzzi that he built himself in the back yard, but instead of using a hose, he thought it would be a great idea to hook into the house's water supply to make his own faucet." Heather waved a hand in dismissal. "They don't have water. I texted Butch to go check it out."

"I'm not sure what worries me more. The he-built-it-himself part, or the tapping-into-a-water-main part," Vivien said. "Do you need to go? I can show Sue upstairs."

"No, Martin is on his way with Jan. He needs to get back to his job site." Heather took a deep breath and looked like she did indeed want to check on the property. "Anyway, I—"

"I can watch Jan," Vivien offered.

Heather hesitated and then shook her head. "No, Butch will text me with pictures."

The front lobby centered around the concessions. Sue recognized the art deco design and gold and burgundy sponge-painted walls from the magazine. Every sign she'd been given had been leading her to this place. The ring sent vibrations up her hand. She could no longer pretend it was too tight and pinching a nerve. The vibrations were too timed, too deliberate.

Something inside her whispered that this was a safe place. Energy pulsed from the walls, nearly imperceptible, and she felt like a young girl walking into a cathedral—the awe, the fear, the power of imprinted human emotions so consuming that it left her speechless.

Muffled voices came from outside. Sue turned to see faces pressed up against the glass as two women looked in at them. Heather started walking toward them, and they quickly went along their way.

"If any busybodies ask what you're doing here, tell them you're theater security," Heather said. "Nobody needs to know your business."

"Tell them to mind their own," Vivien corrected. "I would say to flip them the bird and tell them to fuck off, but you seem nicer than I am."

A small laugh erupted from Sue at the comment. She covered her mouth.

Vivien winked at her. Her phone started ringing in her purse. "This is probably Troy calling me back. Give me a second."

Vivien stepped away to answer the call.

Sue turned to see Heather swatting at the air next to her.

"Bug?" Sue asked, not seeing anything.

"What?" Heather frowned. "Oh, yeah, just a pest."

Sue made a point of glancing around. "This is a great place you have."

"Thank you." Heather again swatted at the air before moving closer to Sue. She gestured to the curtains on either side of the concessions. "The theater seating is through those curtains beside the concession stand. Feel free to wander around if you get bored." She pointed to the right. "Alley access is that way. We keep it locked. My brother has a key to that door, but he'll rarely use it unless I ask him to stop by to do something for me."

Sue nodded.

Heather drew Sue's attention to the left and motioned toward the restroom sign, "restrooms," and then walked past them down a corridor. "This is the office. Concession stand storage is further back. Feel free to grab snacks or sodas from the soda fountain in the lobby. Just leave a note for Lorna so she can track when it's time to reorder more."

Heather stopped at a door near the office and pulled it open to reveal stairs. She gestured that Sue should go ahead of her.

As Sue went up the stairs, Heather followed behind her. "I'll leave you the keys to lock the apartment and to get into the building."

Sue paused near an apothecary cabinet that lined the wall at the top of the stairs. "I can't believe how generous you all are, and all because of a ring I found. I'm sorry if I'm acting standoffish about it all. I'm not used to people being..."

Sue swallowed nervously and fought the tears gathering in her eyes. Heather waited patiently.

"I'm not used to people being kind for no reason," Sue said. "Thank you."

"You're welcome," Heather answered. "I don't know what you've been through, but we're here if you need to talk about it."

Sue nodded, unable to speak as she continued to choke down her emotions.

"I mean, us women of a certain age need to stick together, right?" Heather smiled. "If you ever want to watch something fun, comment to Vivien sometime how life ends for women at forty. Or call yourself old or, like, out-of-date. It will send her on a long, hilarious rant about women empowerment. The last time she did it, there was something in there about magical ovaries shooting sparkles out her hoo-hah—I don't know, but it had us rolling."

Sue chuckled, realizing Heather had intuitively changed the subject to make her feel more at ease. Out of the three ladies, Heather appeared to be the most emotionally guarded, so maybe she understood how difficult it was for Sue to talk about her feelings. "I'll do that."

The loft apartment looked nothing like her home in St. Louis. In fact, it looked like a completely different life. Exposed brick walls had once proudly held the name, "Warrick," but the faded white paint had been scrubbed off the red brick in spots. The faint sound of a revving engine came through the closed windows, moving past on the street below.

As she came to the top, she felt as if she stepped over an invisible threshold between her past and future.

Who was the Sue who stayed in the apartment? What did she want?

This Sue didn't have to have dinner ready at

precisely six o'clock. This Sue didn't have to iron shirts. This Sue didn't have to make sure the towels were folded perfectly, the way her husband liked them. She didn't have to scrub toilets on Tuesday, wash windows on Wednesday, or vacuum daily and make sure the vacuum lines were pointed in the right direction.

What did she want?

With the open floor plan, she could see the entire space from the top of the stairs. Reclaimed wood furniture divided the space into recognizable areas. An island and barstools marked the kitchen's boundaries with a small table next to the window, making a dining area. For the bedroom, there was a queen-size bed, dresser, and nightstand, next to a frosted glass partition. Opened doors revealed a small bathroom and closet. As promised, there was no television, but instead a couch and built-in bookshelf to create the impression of a living room.

"What do you think?" Heather asked. "Will it work?"

"It's perfect," Sue said.

"Good," Heather said. "I've always liked this apartment."

Actually, it was dangerous. A place like this made her want to stay. It made her think that maybe she could walk away from St. Louis and never go back. Perhaps she didn't have to be Susan Jewel anymore.

But that was stupid. She had a house and things that needed her attention.

Could a person start over?

Could she walk away from everything?

Could she pick this location, the here and now, and just... what? Just live in North Carolina? Just move to Freewild Cove, a town she had never heard of until her television started sending her messages from the beyond?

Here, she could disappear. No one knew Hank. She wouldn't have to listen to people tell her how sorry they were, how lucky she'd been, how he was such a wonderful person.

"Yes." Sue nodded, feeling lighter than she had in a long time. "It's perfect. Thank you."

"Have a look around. Please be sure to note that there is a fire ladder under the bed. In case of an emergency, hook it to a window and climb out to the sidewalk below. After some apartment buildings caught fire several years back, I've been making sure to have them in all my properties over one-story."

"Thank you."

"I'm going to go down and wait for Martin and

his daughter. I'd like to introduce you to her." Heather smiled. "She's a special girl."

Sue nodded.

Heather started to go, only to stop. "Do you have kids?"

Sue shook her head. "No. I wanted them, but it wasn't in the cards. You?"

"I had a son," Heather answered.

*Had.*

"I'm sorry." Sue didn't press the issue.

Heather nodded her acknowledgment and hurried down the stairs.

Sue took several deep breaths. There was no sign of Hank's cologne. Maybe this is what the magic had been trying to do, lead her to this place for a new start. Now that it had done that, possibly Hank would be out of her life forever.

This was her future.

Sue found herself smiling as she turned a slow circle to look at the apartment.

What did she want?

Who could she be?

CHAPTER SEVEN

SUE STARED at the quiet street below the apartment window. She wore a pair of pink leggings and a t-shirt with a bedhead kitten on the front. When she threw clothes into the suitcase, she hadn't been paying attention to what she packed. The results were a mismatched wardrobe that would make a bag lady proud.

Streetlights illuminated the night, making it easy to see the view below. For hours, traffic had centered around the Chinese restaurant. She watched the people going in and out—couples, families, groups of friends. The sound of voices occasionally made their way up to her. She watched them, almost mesmerized by the tiny vignette she saw of their lives. A tear slipped down her cheek as she imagined how different this place might be compared to the past.

Sue told herself she was silly for being so fascinated with strangers. She felt as if she stood in a doorway. She could walk all the way through and come out in Freewild Cove, or she could turn around and go back into St. Louis. Both options made her anxious. She wanted a new life so badly. She wanted to forget Mrs. Hank Jewel.

Finally, she realized what she felt was hope.

How long had it been since she'd felt hopeful about anything?

Sue swiped at her tears. She dropped the curtain. Seeing her phone on the charger, she went to check it. She'd found it dead in her purse and hadn't thought to check it sooner. She didn't want to talk to anyone.

Seeing several messages, she contemplated not listening to them.

Sue took the phone to the couch and sat down, crisscrossing her legs, so her feet were off the floor. With a sigh, she put her voice mail on speaker and set her phone on her leg.

*"Sue, this is Kathy. I was thinking of our boy, and I remembered he had these cufflinks that his father*

*had given him. I'd like them back. They have a lot of sentimental value to me. Call me."*

"You mean dollar value," Sue muttered as the call hung up.

*"Sue, this is Kathy. Why haven't you called me? Did you find the cufflinks? I just miss our boy so much. He was such a..."*

Sue frowned at the phone and put her hands over her ears to block the woman's voice. After a few seconds, she dropped her hands and looked down.

*"...a special dinner in his honor. Of course, we expect you to be there, but we won't need you to say anything. I told them you'd be there. I'm going to need you to make sure you clean yourself up. And do your hair. Not like the funeral. Please tell me you've been to a salon. Just call me."*

Sue felt the tension building back in her chest as she touched her hair. In fact, she had not been to a salon. She'd colored her hair with a cheap box from the grocery store. She hated that she felt like she needed to go to the dinner, even when she didn't want to. That old guilt and insecurity ate at her. "No, Kathy, I will not be honoring *our boy.*"

Ugh. She hated when Kathy called him that.

*"Sue, this is Kathy. Why haven't you called? I can't do everything. You need to get in touch with me.*

*There is so much we have to discuss. Oh and did you find the cuff links yet?"*

Sue flipped off the phone.

*"Sue, this is Kathy. Call me."*

*"Sue, this is Kathy. I'm losing my patience. Call me."*

*"Dammit, Sue, this isn't how adults behave. I swear I don't know how my son even put up with you like he did. I told him you were—you need to call me. Do it for Hank. You owe him."*

*"Sue, where the hell are you?"*

Sue gave a small snort of disgust and rubbed the bridge of her nose. "Get a grip, Kathy. It's been like a day."

*"Hello, Mrs. Jewel, this is Officer Hollen from the St. Louis Police Department."*

That caught Sue's attention. She picked up her phone to look at the unfamiliar number.

*"We have some folks here who are very concerned about you. If you get this, please give me a c—"*

There was a pause, and she heard a faint voice in the background. Sue slid the message progress bar back a few seconds and turned up the volume.

Kathy's voice sounded to cut off the officer's, *"You need to look in the river for her. She was never a strong woman. My son was a saint for taking care of her. I told you she was addicted to pain pills, right? And my Hank stood by her the entire time, so patient and loving."*

"Yes, ma'am," the officer said, her tone placating. Then for the message, he finished, *"Please give me a call back on this number anytime."*

Kathy called the police on her because she didn't return a fucking phone call about cuff links?

Even though it was late, Sue dialed the officer's number and began to pace as it rang.

"Officer Hollen," the man answered.

"Uh, yeah, um, hi, Officer Hollen, this is Sue—Susan Jewel. You left me a message that I needed to call you. My phone was dead, and I just charged it." Sue went to the window and glanced out but didn't see what she looked at as she concentrated on the phone call. "I think my mother-in-law might have..."

*...gone insane and called in the cavalry.*

"Yes, hello, Mrs. Jewel. Thank you for getting back to me. You've had us worried."

"I'm sorry. I didn't mean to. Everything's fine. I'm fine."

"I'm glad to hear it. Would it be possible for you to come down to the station for a quick conversation so we can clear this up?" he asked.

"Um, no, I'm sorry. I'm on a small trip right now,"

she answered, dropping the curtain and resuming her pacing. "I'm out of state."

"Where would that be?"

"Freewild Cove, North Carolina. I'm staying with friends," she said. New friends, but friends. It wasn't a lie.

"And when are you expected to return?"

"I'm not sure. It could be awhile."

"Ma'am, are you sure everything is all right? Your mother said you—"

"Mother-in-law," Sue automatically corrected.

"Yes, ma'am, she said that you have been out of contact for a while, and when she let us into your house, she indicated the state of things were not how you normally kept them."

A while? It hadn't even been two freaking days.

"Oh?" Sue frowned, not knowing what state she left the house in. "I mean, I guess I packed really fast."

"The front door was unlocked, and there appeared to have been a struggle," he said. "Can you explain that?"

"I must have been upset." Sue took a deep breath and closed her eyes. With her husband's job, he'd often interacted with police officers. They generally liked him. "My husband just passed away. I needed to get out of the house, so I came to visit friends. I swear everything's fine. I'm fine. I'm just... fine."

"Yes, I found Detective Sanchez's card in your living room. She filled me in on your accident," he said. "After such severe injuries, you can see why we were worried that something worse might have happened to you."

"Well, I'm sorry you were worried. I'm fine," she insisted.

"I'll tell you what. Give me your address, and I'll call Freewild Cove's police department and have them come to check on you, just to be sure. How about that? Then everyone's minds can be put at ease." His tone said he wasn't asking her permission.

"I'm not sure of the address. It's an apartment," she answered, looking around for something that might have an address and not finding anything but the phone numbers Vivien had left her for their cell phones. "Um, just tell them it's the apartment on top of Warrick Theater. It's a small town. They'll know."

"Warrick Theater," he repeated.

"Yes." Sue took another deep breath. Damn Kathy for this.

"Very good. I'll give them a call. Expect someone to come by in the morning," he said.

"Okay, thank you—oh, wait, um, Officer Hollen,

if you don't mind, please don't tell Kathy where I'm staying," Sue said.

"Oh?"

"I mean, I know that sounds dramatic, but it's not. I just, I mean, I came here to get away from things." Sue frowned. She shouldn't have said anything. So what if Kathy found out? "Never mind."

"I won't give her the address, but you should call her. She's very worried about you," Officer Hollen said. "She'll be pleased to know you're safe."

"I'll call her," Sue said.

"Good. I'm happy to hear you're all right, ma'am," Hollen stated. "Expect that visit in the morning."

"Okay, thank you, officer." Sue listened to him hang up and slowly placed her phone on the counter. It took all of one day for her old life to come dragging her back in.

Sue stared at the phone for a long moment. The idea of talking to Kathy left her sick to her stomach. She started to dial, only to stop. Instead, she pulled up text messaging and typed, *"Got your messages. Taking a trip. Phone not holding charge. All good. Talk to you later."*

After sending the message, she lowered the

device's volume and left it face down on the counter. She walked away from the phone and heard it buzz with an incoming call. She checked the screen to make sure it wasn't the police. Seeing it was Kathy, she set it back down and didn't answer.

Sue stepped into her sneakers, walking on the backs of them as the phone continued to vibrate on the countertop. Taking the keys for the building, she went downstairs, pausing mid-step to slip her heels into the shoes.

*Fucking Kathy.*

"Our boy wouldn't want you going out by yourself," Sue mocked the woman under her breath. "Our boy was so great at kicking the shit out of his defenseless wife, wasn't he? Our boy is a real fucking hero with the best cuff links in the world. Don't pawn the cuff links, Sue. I want to."

She pushed open the door to her apartment and didn't bother to lock it behind her. It felt strange standing in the business in the middle of the night.

Sue walked through the lobby and peeked into the empty amphitheater. Rows of seats centered around a black stage and movie screen. Light from the exit signs cast a soft red glow over the area.

She thought of the séances that used to take place, but it didn't frighten her. Those people were long gone and had nothing to do with her. Sue had lived in real fear. A ghost paled next to Hank when he came home drunk and angry.

Unless that ghost was Hank.

Sue shivered. Okay, so maybe she was a little freaked out by the idea of ghosts. She dropped the curtain and walked toward the glass doors in front of the theater. A push bar along the front made it unnecessary to unlock the door from the inside, and she was able to leave.

The evening was chilly but not unbearable. She liked that the downtown was empty. It gave her the chance to explore without overthinking each interaction.

She headed down the block toward where Vivien said there was a coffee shop. It seemed as good of a destination as any. Headlights passed by on the cross street ahead of her. She automatically moved closer to the building, into the shadows, as it passed.

Sue clutched the keys in one hand and dragged the fingers of the other lightly along the building's stone facade. The steady sound of her sneakers on the pavement became pronounced. Thoughts of Kathy's phone calls lingered in the back of her mind, which only gave Hank too much space in her brain.

*"Dammit, Sue! What are you doing going out like that? Are you trying to embarrass me?"*

Sue smoothed her hair back automatically at the memory.

*"Why so shy, baby? Ah, come here, Suzie, dance with your man."*

Hank had been a great dancer. He used to spin her on the dancefloor and take her breath away. Those had been the happy times. That was the thing about her marriage. Not every day had been beatings and yelling. There were moments, really good moments.

"Stop making excuses," Sue scolded herself.

Someone once told her, *"When the bad outweighs the good in a relationship, it's time to get out."*

She should have tried harder to escape.

"Meh."

Sue stopped at the sound and looked around. A white cat sat in the middle of the road, staring at her.

"How are you, little kitty?" Sue asked, slowly approaching the animal.

"Meh," the cat seemed to answer with its strange meow.

"Just meh?" Sue chuckled. "Been there."

As she approached, the cat began to walk away from her. It went to the sidewalk and moved toward the end of the block. Interested in what it might be up to, she followed.

"Hey, kitty, come back," she said in a hushed tone, wanting to pet it. "Do you have a home? What are you doing out here on the street?"

Sue came to the end of the block and turned the corner. A red sedan was parked down the block. The cat kept walking. She kept an eye on the sedan's windows to be sure no one was in there. When she was satisfied the car was empty, she turned her attention to the animal.

The cat sat in front of a glass door. A light came from the back of the quaint bookstore. The animal looked at her and then pawed the door.

"Do you want to go in?"

"Meow."

Sue laughed as the animal answered her. "I'm sorry, it's closed."

Sue pushed on the door handle to show the cat it was locked, but the bookstore door opened. The animal darted inside.

"Oh, crap, stop." Sue let the door close and peered in through the window. The cat strolled through the rows of books and disappeared. It was nearly midnight so going inside, even if the door had accidentally been left unlocked, felt like breaking and entering.

Hey, that would be one way for her to meet the local cops and prove she was alive to St. Louis PD. They could email her mugshot to them. Oh! Or she could send it as the next Christmas card instead of the fake posing happy family. Kathy would *love* that.

Sue chuckled as she imagined the look on the woman's face.

Feeling guilty about letting an animal into someone's store, Sue pulled open the door an inch and said, "Here, kitty, kitty. We shouldn't be in there."

She watched, but the cat didn't come to her.

Sue crouched near the ground to be at the animal's eye level as she searched the back of the store for a sign of where it went. "Here, kitty. Kitty?"

She thought of the life insurance check. Maybe she could go home, call the store, tell them what she did, and offer to pay for any damages. There was some humor in her using it for cat damage since Hank hated cats. Probably because they didn't beg for his attention.

"Lesson learned. Never date a man who hates cats," Sue mumbled, before calling, "Kitty?"

"I love cats," a male voice said from behind her.

Sue inhaled sharply and turned, but from her

precarious position near the ground, her foot slipped, and she fell on her hip. Thankfully, it was a short drop, and it only stung a little. Breathing hard as her heart thumped faster, she looked up.

"Susan Sue." Jameson smiled down at her and offered a hand to help her up. "I see you decided to give our town a chance after all. Though, I will say, it looks better from up here and maybe during the day."

Sue eyed the hand but didn't take it. "I... cat."

"Cat burglar?" Jameson clarified with a playful smile and a glance at her ridiculous bedhead kitten t-shirt.

"No." Sue pushed herself to standing. There was something about this man that made her giddy. The ring vibrated, and she clenched a fist to make it stop. At the gas station, she'd been too exhausted and hungry to recognize the feeling for what it was. She found him extremely attractive, and that made her nervous. If there was anyone whose opinion she couldn't trust when it came to men, it was her own.

Jameson pointed toward the window. "Cat?"

Sue glanced to see the white cat looking out at them from his perch on the window display of books. She wondered how long it had been there staring at her. "The door was unlocked. It wanted to go inside. I was trying to show it that the door was locked, but accidentally opened it, and it ran in."

"*He* ran in," Jameson said. "That's Ace, and the bookstore is his home, well, home base anyway. He kind of comes and goes as he pleases along this block. It's his turf."

Sue released a big sigh and stared at Ace through the window. "I was so sure I was going to be in trouble." She leaned closer to the glass and tapped her finger toward the cat. "You almost made me break into a bookstore, little rascal."

"Meh," Ace answered, indifferent.

"Well, I'm happy I happened to be around," Jameson said. "I saved you from a life of crime."

What were the odds? Sue glanced at the red sedan, realizing it was his car. She hadn't put that fact together until that moment. Red sedans weren't exactly rare.

"Did they ever get the bus fixed?" he asked.

"I assume so." Sue didn't mean for her answer to sound annoyed, but even to her own ears, that's the tone she detected. Forcing some control over her nerves, she said, "I took your recommendation and found that hotel. Thank you for pointing me in the right direction."

"If it were me, I'd call the company and demand

a refund." Jameson smiled. "And ask for reimbursement for the hotel room. It's the least they could do for stranding you in the middle of the night. And if they say no, they say no."

"Yeah, thanks, I'll think about it." Sue stayed near the bookstore door.

Jameson appeared to notice and stepped back on the sidewalk to give her space.

"What are you doing out here at this time of night?" she asked, trying to think of anything to fill the growing silence.

He gestured to his left. "Inventory. I could ask you the same thing."

"Exploring," she answered. Sue took a step forward to look at the store he indicated. "You work at the coffee shop?"

Jameson nodded. "More or less. I own it."

"Own?" Sue glanced at the shop again and inched closer to peek inside.

The window read, "*The Coffee Shop in Freewild Cove.*" Sue looked at the bookstore. That window read, "*The Bookstore in Freewild Cove.*"

"Um, clever shop titles," she said.

"It's been great for internet searches. They say what they are," he said.

"So, do you own the bookstore, too?"

"Just the building. Melba owns the shop."

"And Ace?"

"I don't think anyone can own Ace. He's a free spirit." Jameson chuckled.

"What made you decide to join the barista arts?" she asked, trying to sound clever.

"As a young lad, it was always my wish to remain highly sugared and caffeinated," Jameson joked. "This gave me the perfect excuse."

Sue couldn't help but laugh. "Living the dream, huh?"

"Exactly." He gestured toward the door. "Want to come in?"

Sue started to shake her head in denial, but the ring sent a little jolt up her arm, and she found herself saying, "Yes, as long as I'm not interrupting."

"Not at all. You can watch me count tea boxes." Jameson held open the coffee shop door for her. "It's fascinating work."

Sue glanced at Ace, who paused to look at her from where he licked his erect back leg.

"I'll leave the door unlocked. You can go at any time," Jameson said. "I understand if you don't want to be alone at night with a stranger in a strange town."

Instead of answering, Sue pointed toward the

bookstore and said, "Should we try to lock that door, so no one breaks in?"

"Melba doesn't always remember to lock up." He motioned upward. "I have a camera that covers both entrances. If something happens, we'll see it."

Sue looked up to see the small camera. "That's how you knew I was out here?"

He nodded.

"Is there a lot of crime here? I noticed the theater had security cameras too," she said.

"Not really. Usually, drunk tourist stupidity and most of that is closer to the beach. I got the camera more so I could make sure the morning shift shows up on time. Stu's a great guy but often imbibes in drunk local stupidity. He's plays gigs down at the beach, then comes in here and works the morning shift." Jameson chuckled. "Ah, to be young again."

"Did you just imply that we're old?" Sue arched a brow at him as she walked into the coffee shop.

Was she flirting?

"Never." He grinned. "You don't look a day over eighteen."

"Please tell me that isn't true," she said. "You couldn't pay me to be a teenager again. I'll accept a day over thirty, which is a lie, but a nicer lie."

"Thirty it is," he said. "I'm forty-seven, by the

way. So I guess that makes me the old man."

"Hardly." She paused to look around the shop. A light came from a back room. He flipped on a light switch. "I'm forty if we're disclosing."

Saying her age made her think of her birthday. She closed her eyes and took a deep breath.

"I love the smell of this place," he said, misreading what she was doing.

His comment turned her attention back to the shop. The smell of ground coffee permeated the air. It was a great smell. Wood plank walls enclosed the narrow space, or at least from what she saw of the walls from behind the paintings. Almost every inch was covered. Rows of homemade jelly had been stacked into a kiosk next to a matching display holding tea tins. Pyramids displays towered higher than most customers could reach and showcased coffee cups with the store logo and soy candles. Handcrafted jewelry had been set up by the register.

"It's a great shop. You have a little of everything," Sue said.

"Thanks. I can't take credit for everything. Most of it is here on consignment. The paintings, jewelry, and candles all come from local artists. A lady makes the jams to supplement her retirement. On busy days, she sells baked goods. A ceramist outside of town makes the mugs for me. A kid at the High School screen-prints the t-shirts." He smiled. "I love that it's become a sort of artistic beacon for the town. We even had a hand-drawn greeting card vending machine out front for a time, but the guy who owned it moved and took it with him."

Maybe it was the smell of coffee and candle wax that gave the impression of coziness, but the shop felt homey and safe.

"Sue?"

Sue blinked and turned to him, realizing she hadn't been listening. "I'm sorry, what did you say?"

"I asked if you wanted some coffee. Nothing fancy, but I have a pot on," he said.

"Coffee at midnight?" Sue thought for a moment and then smiled. "Why not? We're adults, aren't we? We can do whatever we want."

Jameson grinned as he went around the counter and poured her a cup. He set it down.

"Oh, I don't have—" Sue didn't bring her wallet.

"It's a gift." He lifted his mug toward her. "To living dangerously and drinking coffee at midnight."

"To living dangerously." Sue placed the keys on the counter and then lifted her mug to take a sip. At the last minute, she stiffened, worried that it might taste like liquor. Thankfully, it didn't. For a moment, she'd been able to forget who she was. "Delicious, thank you."

Jameson set his mug down and slapped his hand lightly on the counter. "Okay, back to counting."

He lifted a remote from behind the register and pointed it at a stereo. Instantly, classic rock sounded over the store speakers. He disappeared into the office only to return with a clipboard.

"I thought this is why bosses had employees," Sue said, leaning against the counter as she drank her coffee.

"Stu had a gig tonight," Jameson answered. "I don't mind. It only takes a few hours."

Jameson went to the teas and began counting tins by pointing his pen at them. He moved it in time with the music, and she wondered if he was aware that he kept the beat.

When he paused to write down a number, Sue approached. "You're right. This is fascinating work."

Jameson laughed.

"Not to brag but I happen to be an excellent counter," she said.

"Oh, yeah?" He grinned.

Sue nodded.

He motioned toward the coffee mug pyramid. "Mugs?"

"On it, boss." She gave a small salute.

"I see, you're trying to muscle Stu out of a job." Jameson laughed.

"Not if that means the morning shift." Sue went to the pyramid display. "I'm a midnight coffee girl now."

"So what do you do, if I can ask?"

"I..." Sue furrowed her brow. "I don't know. I guess I'm looking for work."

"Oh yeah? What are you looking for?"

"I'm not sure." She grinned. "Cat burglar, maybe? I have the shirt for it."

Jameson nodded, laughing as he tapped his pen against the clipboard. "Fair enough."

They fell into a comfortable silence as they both counted. When she finished the mugs, she started on candles, then moved to jams. Soon they were working their way around the entire store, counting inventory, drinking coffee, dancing and singing softly to classic rock. Once, Jameson even took her hand, twirling her to the music as he walked past her.

"And we're done," Jameson said, standing up from the floor. He crossed to the counter and put the clipboard down. "Thank you for your help."

"No problem, I actually had fun."

"Actually?" Jameson chuckled. "Don't sound so

surprised."

"Oh, no, I didn't mean it like that. I've enjoyed doing inventory." Sue slowly followed him to the counter. "I've just had a rough few months, and this was..." She looked around the store. "It's been nice not having to think about it."

"Anything you want to talk about?"

Sue shook her head.

Jameson walked around to the back of the counter and reached under the register. He pulled out a loyalty card and began punching it with a coffee cup-shaped hole puncher. When he finished, he signed his name on the back and handed it to her. "I think you earned this free latte."

Sue liked that he didn't pressure her to talk. Whenever they hit a sensitive topic, he sensed it and changed the subject. Conversation with him flowed, but even more importantly, silence with him was easy.

Sue detected the kindness in him. After years of Hank, she'd become an expert at spotting meanness in people. She didn't always trust herself, but with Jameson, she felt she could trust him.

Sue took the card from him and grinned. "Thank you. I think I'll come back in the morning and get that latte. I kind of want to meet Stu."

"Into the younger guys?" He teased as he put the hole puncher away, but she saw the curiosity in his expression as he listened for her answer.

"No." Sue laughed, and he looked relieved. "Musicians."

"Oh." Jameson's head tilted back as he laughed, the sound welcoming. "I guess I better dust off my guitar before I ask you out."

The ring on her hand tingled as if prompting her to pick up the offer. "Couldn't hurt."

Jameson took their coffee mugs and carried them to a sink. "I'll remember that."

"I should be getting back." Sue started backing up toward the door.

"I didn't see a car outside. You need a ride somewhere?"

"Heather Harrison is letting me stay at the movie theater," Sue said.

"You're staying in the theater?" He quirked a brow.

"The apartment, upstairs," she corrected.

"Ah." Jameson kept his eyes steadily on her. For a moment, she thought he might offer to walk her home. "Then I guess I'll be seeing you around the neighborhood."

Even though she was a little disappointed when

he didn't, it was probably for the best. Walking someone home felt too much like the end of a date.

Sue picked up her keys from the counter and lifted the card to give him a small wave. "Thanks for this."

"Thanks for your help." Jameson watched her leave.

Once outside, she moved from his eyesight and let loose a long breath, and grinned as she danced in a little circle. Ace still sat in the bookstore window, watching her. She tapped her finger on the glass and said, "I owe you one, buddy."

Then remembering the security camera watching the area, she ducked her head in embarrassment and hurried down the sidewalk and around the corner. Once she was out of sight of the security camera, she stopped. Her heartbeat quickly, and she had a hard time catching her breath. At first, she thought it might be a panic attack, but she was too happy.

Giddy. She felt giddy, like a freaking teenager waiting for a prom date.

It had been such a long time since she'd been excited that the feeling almost eluded her. For so long, she'd been living day to day, moment to moment, focused only on survival.

Was the house clean enough?

Would the food be done on time?

Did she have enough time to fix her makeup before the oven timer went off and Hank came home?

Moment to moment, every one of them scheduled. Day to day, each one formulated to make someone else happy. But was Hank ever really happy? He had some kind of demon in him, one that drove him to drink, one that made him care too much about appearances.

Already she could see Jameson was not like that. He didn't check his appearance in reflective surfaces. He didn't constantly straighten his clothes. She hadn't noticed such little things on those first dates with Hank that came to mean so much.

Her marriage had not been love. It had been a prison sentence, a dark hole without air, without windows or light, without hope. The idea of going back to St. Louis, of stepping back into that house, terrified her. She couldn't walk back into the cell. She couldn't talk to Kathy and hear the woman praise her captor. She couldn't smile while people told her how great a guy Hank had been, how she was one of the lucky ones.

It proved people didn't know the pain others

carried. They saw a façade. They saw what they needed to see for their lives to make sense. But there was no such thing as a perfect couple, a perfect family, an ideal life. There were always secrets.

Thoughts of her past dampened her spirits. Would she ever escape the voices in her head? She wished there was a way to sever the thread leading to her memories.

Sue paused at the theater door to unlock it.

*"You should be ashamed of wearing that ridiculous outfit in public."*

Sue gasped, dropping the key on the sidewalk. She turned, expecting to see her dead husband behind her. The street was empty.

Headlights passed on the cross street, and she assumed Jameson was leaving work. She took a deep breath. It was late and thinking of her past had made her jumpy.

Sue's hands shook as she picked up the keys. She gave a short laugh and tried to dismiss the nervousness. "Maybe midnight coffee wasn't the best idea."

*"You think I don't know what's in that head of yours?"* The sound of Hank's whisper was joined by the unmistakable smell of his bourbon breath. *"Wishing you could spread your legs like a whore for any man who smiles at you."*

Sue gave a small yelp of panic and fumbled to unlock the door. As she pushed inside, she saw the faintest reflection of Hank's face in the glass. Sunken, dark eyes glared at her.

Sue screamed as she stumbled inside. The weighted door slowly pulled itself closed. She stared through the glass at the sidewalk beyond.

Breathing heavily, she was too afraid to move. She didn't take her eyes from the door. She knew what she saw. The image of Hank's face lingered even when it no longer showed in the glass.

"I'm not crazy. I know what was there. I'm not crazy," she whispered. "It's all real. Ghosts are real."

The smell of the cologne did not follow her inside, but still, she couldn't force herself to move away from the doors. Who did a person call in a situation like this? The police? They'd think she was mental.

Sue glanced briefly at the security camera and then back to the sidewalk. She waved her hand frantically, hoping to get Vivien, Heather, or Lorna's attention while not taking her eyes away from the door. The odds of them being awake were slim. After several seconds, she turned toward the camera only long enough to mouth, "Help me."

# CHAPTER EIGHT

"SHE'S HERE!" Vivien's announcement came from behind.

Sue screamed in fright at the sudden voice, grabbing her chest. She'd been searching each tiny reflection in the theater's front door for so long, lost in fear, that she hadn't heard them come from the alley entrance.

"Oh, hey, easy, easy," Lorna soothed as she rushed toward her. She wrapped her arms around her shoulders. "We're here just like we told you we would be."

"I'll check the theater," Heather stated.

"I got the back rooms," Vivien added.

Both women hurried to their self-assigned tasks.

"What happened?" Lorna asked.

Sue pointed a shaking hand at the door. "I saw..."

"What? What did you see?" Lorna hugged her tighter, and Sue started feeling a little better.

"Hank," Sue finished.

"You saw your dead husband? Where?" Lorna looked around the lobby.

"I went for a walk outside, and when I came back to unlock the door, I smelled him, then I heard him, and then I saw him in the glass." Sue took a steadying breath. "Reflected in the glass."

"But nowhere else?" Lorna kept her voice calm.

Sue shivered. "I don't know. I came in and watched, but I didn't see him come in."

"Storage room and office are clear," Vivien said. "I can go check upstairs."

"No, Viv." Lorna stopped her and pointed toward the doors. "He was outside."

"He? The husband?" Vivien asked.

"Do we have to keep calling him that?" Sue whispered. "As far as I'm concerned, my vows ended at 'til death do us part and not a second longer."

"We can call him whatever you want," Vivien stated. "I'm partial to the asshat, but asshole, twat waffle, and little fuckety-fuck-fuck, all work too."

To her surprise, Sue laughed. She hadn't thought anything could make her feel better after seeing

Hank, but somehow these women had. It was then she realized that both Vivien and Lorna wore pajamas. Vivien had on shorts under a bathrobe and sneakers, and Lorna wore flannel pants and fuzzy slippers.

"Did you see me on the camera?" Sue asked.

"I had Troy set up a motion alarm to alert us if anything happened in the lobby. He's a college professor in charge of setting up the online curriculum for—it doesn't matter right now. He's all about the tech. Anyway, I saw you go out for a walk earlier, and then it woke me when you came back. I promised you we'd be here for you."

As creepy as the big brother thing was, Sue was grateful in this instance.

"Come to think of it, that was one long walk you took," Vivien said. "Where did you go?"

Sue thought of Jameson.

"Is that...? Are you turning red?" Vivien grinned. "Oh, please tell me you were out on a booty call."

"What? No!" Sue shook her head. "I just arrived in Freewild Cove. I don't know anyone. Who would I booty call with?"

"Um, I've never found the length of time to be an issue," Vivien said. "If you want booty, there is someone who will call for it. Trust me, a beautiful woman of experience like you? No question. You can get plenty of booty."

"Stop saying the word booty," Lorna mumbled.

"Booty-booty," Vivien teased.

"Woman of experience? Is that a nice way of saying I look old?" Sue glanced down at her cat shirt. "Because I feel old and frumpy."

"Hell no," Vivien said. "Forty isn't old. You're just getting started baby!"

When Sue began to ask how she knew her age, Vivien cut her off.

"Yeah, we looked at your driver's license when you passed out," Vivien confessed, not sounding sorry. "We were trying to make sure you didn't have any medical alert cards or medication you needed in your purse. So, as I was saying, forty isn't old. These are our years of perfection. We're experienced enough to know our minds. All that drama that comes with youth no longer matters. So what if my ass has an extra few pounds? It's a great ass."

"Uh, I think that's my line," Lorna interrupted with a laugh.

"Yours is a great ass too," Vivien said.

"Thanks." Lorna shook her head, more amused by the speech than anything.

"Where was I?" Vivien asked.

"Great asses," Lorna prompted.

"Right. Sue, you're not old. You're a seasoned professional at this thing we call life." Vivien circled a finger in the air and struck a sassy pose.

"Is Viv doing her ode to sparkling vaginas again?" Heather appeared from behind the curtain. Like the others, she was in pajamas—a long flannel nightshirt and leggings with black house shoes.

"No, tonight we all have great extra-pound asses," Lorna answered.

"Ah. Good to know." Heather chuckled.

Vivien grinned and said, "Now that you mention it, there is nothing wrong with a little bedazzling on the—"

"And on that note," Lorna interrupted. "How about we get back to the matter at hand? We're here for Sue. I'm sure she has questions."

"Why is this happening?" Sue instantly asked now that they had refocused. She looked at each of them in turn.

"That's an excellent question." Heather motioned that they should follow her. "I'm set up if you're ready."

"Set up for what?" Sue asked.

"To see if we can't find out why this is happening

to you," Vivien said, turning Sue's question back on her.

Lorna tried to walk Sue toward the amphitheater.

"Do you mean a séance?" Sue asked, refusing to budge. "I thought you didn't do that here anymore."

"Not publicly," Vivien stated. "We still do them. Don't worry. We're getting pretty good at it, and summoning Julia is a fairly safe bet. We were going to wait a few days until you settled in, but considering tonight's paranormal activity, it's probably best to get this show on the road."

"Fairly?" Sue clung to that one word.

"We're going to call Grandma Julia so all of you can see her," Heather said. "I could ask her and translate, but I think maybe this is something you need to hear for yourself. Seeing is believing, after all."

"Julia Warrick?" Sue shivered, rubbing her arms.

"The one and only." Heather went back behind the curtain.

"I'm going to grab candy out of the storeroom for after," Vivien said, leaving the lobby.

"It's safe," Lorna assured her. "Julia doesn't mean us harm. If her magic sent you the ring, then she means for you to be here. She's tied to this place, so I think that makes her stronger when we call to her here," Lorna said.

"I..." Sue wasn't sure what she thought. On the one hand, she didn't want to see Hank ever again—spirit or not. On the other, she didn't want to call more ghosts into her life.

"I know," Lorna soothed. The woman definitely had a nurturing quality to her. She slid her hands off of Sue's shirt to touch her forearms. The skin-to-skin contact connected them just as it had with Vivien.

The prickling sensation of awareness started where they touched. It shivered over her and caused goosebumps to rise on her arms and legs. She felt her hair lifting like the effect of static electricity.

"We know you're scared," Lorna said.

Sue nodded. That was an understatement.

"When this was happening to me, when I tried to get closure after my husband died, I was terrified. I wasn't like Vivien or Heather. I was like you. I didn't grow up knowing ghosts existed, or magic, or mediums, or any of this. It was a fantasy story or Hollywood movie. Heather sees ghosts like Julia. Vivien is psychic like her ancestors." Lorna held up her ring. "Until I put this on, I was just a sad lady whose husband had cheated on her in the worst way."

Sue looked at her ring. "I didn't ask for this."

"You didn't have to." Lorna leaned over to force Sue to look at her. "But Julia's magic knew you needed it. You might not want it, but you needed it. And there are strange perks."

"Are you coming?" Heather called.

"We need a moment," Lorna answered.

Sue put her hand over Lorna's on her arm. She felt the woman's sincerity. Her energy was different than Vivien's. Lorna was gentle, a mother, a nurturer. Beneath that was an echo of her old pain. It would be a scar she carried with her, but it had dulled and healed over.

"I'm not going to lie." Lorna tightened her hands on Sue's arms. "It's going to break your heart to face this, but when it's over, the healing is worth it. You'll see life is not him. It was never meant to be like him. You were meant for more. I can feel that in you. You were meant to love and be loved."

"What did you mean by perks?" Sue heard Vivien coming back from the storeroom.

"The rings amplify something inside us. For me, I desire to take care of others, my family, and my friends. It's all I ever wanted to do. As a mother, I could always find anything in the house. I never thought of it as a skill, but with the ring, I have the natural magic to find lost things. And, as we talked about before, I'm a healer. I can transfer physical illness and injury from one to another or into myself. I don't like that as much. I don't like making those decisions."

Sue shook her head. "I don't have any natural magic. I'm not good at anything."

"I don't believe that's true." Lorna released her arm. "You might not see it yet, but you have something inside you."

"Come in when you're ready, but do come in." Lorna walked behind the curtain.

Sue felt colder without the contact. She rubbed her arm where Lorna had touched her. She doubted she had natural magic. What was she good at? Keeping secrets? Following orders to avoid punishment? Cleaning?

*Magical punching bag maid,* she thought in dejection.

"Stop that nonsense," Vivien whispered as she passed.

Sue glanced at her in surprise.

Vivien gave her a sad smile. "Never again."

Sue slowly nodded.

"Good." Vivien walked toward the curtains holding an armful of movie theater candy boxes.

Sue checked the dark sidewalk beyond the glass

door. Hank wasn't there. How easy it would be to tell herself she imagined it.

She wasn't one to lie to herself, even when she'd justified her bad decisions. Would walking into the theater to perform a séance be another regret? Or would she regret walking away from the help and friendship these women offered?

Beyond practical matters and fear, curiosity stirred. Ghosts? How often did a person get the chance to see proof of the supernatural, of an afterlife?

Sue found herself walking toward the curtain. Although she knew it to be thick, hanging material, she felt it was more like a veil, another threshold between her past and her future. If she stepped through, it took her further away from who she had been.

Sue ran her hand along the red velvet, feeling the soft texture even as she detected the faintest hint of age and dust. She should want to run from her past, but the future scared her too.

Everything scared her.

She hated that fear.

Sue wasn't sure what she expected to see when she balled her fist around the material and pulled the curtain aside. Her eyes went first to the lit stage where Vivien, Heather, and Lorna waited, then to the theater seats hidden in the shadows. There couldn't be more than a hundred cushioned seats, but she scanned over each one as she walked down the aisle, half expecting an audience of ghosts to stare back at her.

She took several deep breaths before finally focusing on the stage. Lorna sat on the stage, digging through a messenger bag. They'd spread a blue cloth on the floor. When Sue went up the stairs along the stage's edge, she saw that a thick, old book had been placed in the middle of the cloth. A symbol had been drawn on the fabric to match the symbol on the book's cover.

Lorna pulled out blue candles, dropped oil on them from a vial, and handed them to Vivien.

"What are you doing?" Sue asked, approaching hesitantly.

"Anointing the candles with basil oil. It's for protection. And the blue will amplify our message to Julia," Lorna suddenly frowned. "I don't have blue-berries."

"It's just Julia," Vivien dismissed as she arranged the four blue candles at the edge of the cloth but didn't light them. "We'll be all right."

"Blueberries?" Sue asked.

"They help against psychic attacks," Vivien said.

"Antioxidants of the supernatural world." Lorna went behind the theater screen and returned with four pillows tucked under her arms. She placed them on the floor behind the candles. Seeing Sue watching her, she chuckled. "For our backsides," she glanced to Vivien and grinned, "padded as they might be with the extra sexy, age-positive poundage. My hips do not take kindly to sitting on hard floors like they used to."

"And the book?" Sue gestured to the giant tome in the center of the whatever-it-was they were creating.

"Family heirloom." Heather sat on a pillow. She suppressed a yawn, reminding Sue how late it was. "It belonged to Julia."

"I'm sorry, we haven't thought about the best way to explain everything to people—not that we were expecting that we'd have to explain it, I guess." Lorna frowned at the display. "This whole altar thing must look odd."

Sue nodded.

"There's a lot to this, too much to go over right now, but I'll try to give you the fast version. We found the book hidden under this stage. It has directions on how to do seances, logs of people Julia helped, and ways we can protect ourselves—like the blueberries and basil oil." Lorna gestured to encompass the design on the cloth. "This symbol usually locks the spirits inside. Not Julia, but others. See how the symbols look like our rings?" Lorna pointed at the fabric and then held up her hand to show her ring.

Sue looked at her hand and then the cloth. She didn't see her symbol but knew hers matched a pattern on the outside of the theater.

"Without the cloth, the spirits become trapped on top of the book cover and aren't able to move around." Lorna took a seat next to Heather. "They don't like it as much. This is better."

Sue had many questions but doubted the answers would put her at ease. Asking them would only delay the inevitable of going through with it.

Vivien sat across from Lorna, leaving one open spot for Sue.

"Do we need to light the candles?" Sue sat on the pillow with her back toward the seats, thankful she wasn't expected to stand.

"Oh, here," Vivien reached for the book and flipped the cover open. Handwritten in calligraphy, the word *"Warrick"* appeared on the title page. She took out a piece of paper and laid it in front of Sue. "You can read off that when we start."

"This first part is pretty neat," Heather said as

she joined hands with the other two. Louder, as if to the entire theater, she stated, "We intend to talk to Julia Warrick."

Vivien and Lorna held their hands toward Sue. She slowly took them, completing the circle. At the contact, a zap of energy flowed through her from one set of joined hands into the other. Instantly, the candle wicks caught fire without anyone moving to light them.

"Holy crap." Sue gasped and tried to pull away but Vivien and Lorna, clearly having anticipated as much, held tight.

"Consider that a warmup." Vivien grinned.

The rush of emotion coming at her from the other women was almost too much. Her heart beat faster, and she found herself trying to catch her breath. At the same time, her own fears and pain seemed to leave her, flowing out of her into her new friends as if they tried to take on some of her burdens. The energy built until the static charge caused her hair to lift from her shoulders. She looked at the others, seeing they suffered the same effects.

As she looked at them, the feelings deepened. Sue began to understand these women as if they were part of her.

Vivien ran headfirst into life, embracing every

second. With her psychic abilities, she had a built-in defense mechanism. She detected danger and avoided it. She also used her powers to fiercely protect the people she cared about.

Lorna had a softer energy. Her compassion was anchored deep to the point she would put everyone else's needs before her own. She'd give her last dollar to a stranger in need.

Heather had been a more challenging read, but the connection opened the woman up a little more. She carried her emotions close, hiding behind a mask to hide the pain she carried, burying it in endless work. It was an old pain, one she'd accepted, but that still radiated with an ache that could never go away.

Sue gasped, trying to catch her breath. She'd worked so hard to hide herself, never to let anyone see her waver. With the rush of emotions in, it only stood to reason that her feelings went out. As she understood the mysteries of those around her, so too were they reading her secrets. A tear slipped down her face. She waited to feel their judgment.

Why did she stay with Hank?

How could she not have known the man she married?

How could any self-respecting woman put up with so much?

"That son of a bitch," Vivien swore.

Heather stared at her from across the circle. "Trust me. When we're done talking to Julia, we're going to come up with a plan to summon that pitiful excuse for a human and give him an ass-kicking deep into a hell that he won't ever escape."

"No one would have been able to see that kind of evil," Lorna said. "The devil is good at hiding himself, Sue. It's not your fault, none of it."

Sue cried harder, nodding.

They didn't judge her. They supported her. They believed her and she hadn't needed to say a word.

No one had ever believed her.

For so long, everyone saw what Hank wanted them to see. They loved him. They looked at her like she wasn't worthy of such a good and charming man. If she tried to talk about something even minor that he'd done, they'd frown in censure and accuse her of being dramatic.

"Thank you," Sue whispered, the words catching.

"Let's do this," Vivien said.

"Our intention is to talk to Julia Warrick," Heather announced again. The bright lights over the stage flickered. Sue looked up and then around.

138

"It's okay. Spirits need energy to manifest," Lorna said. "It's better she takes it from the lights than from us."

Lorna nodded toward the paper on the floor in front of Sue.

The three women said in unison, "Spirits tethered to this plane we humbly seek your guidance. Spirits search amongst your numbers for the spirit we seek. We call forth Julia Warrick from the great beyond."

Sue read along silently. Vivien squeezed her hand and nodded that she should speak.

"Spirits tethered to this plane," they began again, and Sue joined in, "we humbly seek your guidance. Spirits search amongst your numbers for the spirit we seek. We call forth Julia Warrick from the great beyond."

They all paused and glanced around.

"Heather, do you see her?" Vivien asked.

Heather shook her head in denial. "No, I don't know where..."

A tiny giggle sounded from the theater seats, followed by running footsteps.

"Did you all hear that?" Vivien asked.

"Yeah," Heather said.

"How did a kid get in here?" Lorna broke hand

contact and stood. She walked to the side of the stage. "Hello? Who's there? Come out, please."

Heather stood. Vivien let go of her hand, and Sue turned to look behind her. The pillow turned with her as she remained on the ground.

"I said come out, please," Lorna stated in an unmistakable mom tone. She placed her hands on her hips. Lorna and Vivien joined her. Sue stayed on the pillow, nervously watching. The lights continued to flicker.

"Shit, you don't think we stirred a lost child spirit, do you?" Vivien asked. "I hate when they're young. It's always so sad."

A cool blast hit the side of Sue's neck. "Your soul is dusty, and you smell like death."

Sue yelped and hurried away from the voice. By the time her eyes managed to focus, she was stumbling to her feet. A young girl in an extremely out-of-date dress stood on the stage—or rather, maybe she floated on the stage since Sue could see through her transparent figure. Dark brown hair had been curled in ringlets and tied with a red bow.

"There you are," Lorna said, leaning over to be more on the girl's level even though she was several feet away. "What's your name, sweetheart?"

The girl's face scrunched up in defiance. "It sure as hell ain't sweetheart!"

Lorna gasped and stood up straight.

"Grandma Julia," Heather said, her tone wry. "Would you mind growing up a little?"

"Do I look like a grandma to you?" the ghost challenged. She might be wearing a cute dress, but she looked ready to throw down in a fight.

Sue tried to remain calm. This was a ghost.

*A freaking ghost.*

*A real live—well not live—ghost.*

*Crap. Breathe, Sue, breathe. Don't freak out.*

*In. Out. In. Out.*

"Fine. Julia," Heather said, her tone exasperated. "You do not look like a grandma right now. I thought we talked about this. When I séance you, I need you to come to us older and more mature."

"I don't have to listen to you. You're not my mother. I come as I need to come." Julia laughed, a creepy, ghostly sound, as she began hopscotching invisible squares on the stage. She got to the end and turned back around to do it again.

Vivien reached a hand to Sue on the ground to help her up. "Yeah, sorry about this. Julia sometimes manifests younger than she died. I've never seen her this young, though. Heather will try to get her on track for us so we can talk to her."

"That's, ah, that's..." Sue pointed weakly at the spirit.

"A ghost, yeah," Vivien said. "Freaking awesome, right?"

"Ghost," Sue managed to finish her breathy sentence.

"She's a quick one," Julia teased.

None of this is what Sue had expected.

"Julia, please, we need your help. Older you," Heather pleaded.

"The clues are there, so simple," Julia answered, her voice singsongy. She stumbled to a stop. "You make me lose my place!"

"Why don't you tell us the clues if you're so smart," Lorna challenged the spirit. "Or is it you don't know?"

"Good one," Vivien said under her breath.

Julia began skipping around the stage, circling Lorna. "You smell me with your nose. You taste me with your tongue—"

"Is this some kind of riddle?" Lorna asked.

Julia moved from Lorna to Heather, circling her as well. "You hear me with your ears." She then skipped around Vivien. "You see me with your eyes."

"Thanks for stating the obvious," Vivien said.

Stopping, Julia looked at Sue and hunched over. She curled her fingers and took stuttering steps toward Sue. Her transparent body flicked with the lights. Her tone darkened and became raspy, "But when I touch you, you'll know the feel of death —*ahh!*"

Julia lurched toward Sue, blasting over her like a cold breeze.

Sue lifted her arms to block the attack, but when Julia moved through her, she felt as if her insides froze. She let out a pained whimper. Her breath escaped her in a puff of white.

"Julia!" Heather scolded. "Enough!"

"What?" Julia giggled. "I'm only playing with her."

"Grow up, or I swear I will ignore you until the end of time," Heather threatened. "I'll lock up this theater, board up the windows, and no one will ever come in again. See how boring everything is then."

Shivering, Sue turned to see child Julia shimmer into sparkling lights before she disappeared.

"Damn, Julia was a brat as a kid," Vivien said. "I don't believe in spanking, but—"

"Don't make me curse, Vivien," a woman warned. "Don't judge until you walked a mile in my childhood slippers. It wasn't easy for a girl at that time, especially a girl who saw ghosts and wanted to be more than a socialite wife."

Sue swung around to face another Julia ghost. The young woman wore high-waisted trousers with a button-down shirt and vest with a dangling gold chain coming from a pocket. The clothes combined with the wavy bob and red lipstick said she was dressed for the 1920s. She lifted her hand and a lit cigarette appeared at the end of a long holder. She brought it to her lips and the smoke seemed to swirl lightly within her translucent chest.

Julia made a point of cocking her hip to the side as she looked around the theater. "You ask a gal to show, but you don't bother to bring me anything worth looking at. Where's that boyfriend of yours?" Julia grinned at Heather. "That one has a backside a girl can—"

"No, Grandma," Heather interrupted.

Sue held very still, happy the spirit wasn't paying attention to her. She wished she could fade into the shadows and hide until it was over.

*In. Out. In. Out.*

"Ah, let her talk," Vivien said. "Martin does have a great ass. Must be all that heavy lifting."

Julia laughed.

Lorna moved to stand closer to Sue. She turned her back on the ghost and said softly, "Just humor 1920s Julia. She's a handful but won't hurt you."

Julia didn't appear to hear Lorna. She gravitated closer to Vivien. She seemed to float more than walk even though her legs moved. The cigarette disappeared. "That looker of yours isn't hard on the peepers, either."

"I'll tell him you said so," Vivien said.

"Do better than that. Next time you summon me, make sure you bring me something to look at. I may be dead, but I'm not *dead*." Julia winked and laughed. "Oh, see if you can get him to take a shower upstairs."

Sue watched the interaction, tucking her head a little and drawing her arms in to make herself small. This definitely wasn't anything close to what she'd been expecting. She thought maybe there would be a white misty figure floating around, moaning warnings. Julia was vibrant and lucid.

That didn't make her any less scary, though.

*In. Out. In. Out.*

Sue stayed motionless, praying Julia didn't single her out again.

*In. Out—*

It wasn't to be.

Julia turned to face Sue and smiled. "So you brought me another."

Sue glanced to Heather and then back again.

"Julia, this is Sue Jewel. She just arrived in Freewild Cove," Heather introduced. "Sue, this is Julia Warrick, my sometimes grandmother depending on her age."

"Does the kitten speak?" Julia asked.

"I..." Sue swallowed. "Yes."

Julia pointed a finger close to her face. Sue leaned away.

"Boo!" Julia exclaimed.

Sue jumped in fright.

Julia laughed. "That never gets old."

"Julia, behave," Heather said in exasperation. "It's late. We're all exhausted. Please try to focus."

"Hmm." Julia hooked her thumbs into her pockets and slowly walked around Sue, examining her. "You found a ring?"

"Uh, yes, ma'am," Sue answered.

"Show me your paw, kitten," Julia ordered.

Sue held up a shaking hand to show her.

Julia leaned in to look at it. She reached for Sue's hand. Icy prickles brushed against her skin and sent a shiver down Sue's arm.

"Ah, yeah, that makes sense now," Julia said.

"That's why you look like you've already been fitted for a Chicago overcoat. If you're not careful, the tailor is going to finish it, you understand?"

Sue shook her head in denial. She didn't understand. Not at all. She rubbed her cold hand.

"What's a Chicago overcoat?" Heather asked.

Julia frowned. "A little sensitivity, doll, please."

The scolding sounded odd coming from the brash spirit.

"Does Sue's ring mean something in particular?" Lorna asked.

"Can't you see it?" Julia turned to Vivien. "Her aura looks like someone took a bat to it."

Sue stiffened and hugged her arms to her stomach.

"I don't see auras," Vivien said.

"Oh, not yet? Sorry, I must be ahead of myself. Time when you're dead is a funny thing." Julia sighed. "It's dusty, bruised, but it looks like there's a little," Julia gestured to Sue's breasts, "spot of something there."

Sue glanced down at her chest to the bedhead kitten.

"A guy, perhaps? First stirrings of love?" Julia arched a brow. "Makes sense with that ring and your particular problem. You need to learn to trust yourself. Not an easy thing, harder for you than most."

"I knew it!" Vivien exclaimed as if she couldn't help herself. "You met a guy tonight, didn't you?"

"Viv, not the time," Heather chided.

"Well?" Julia came closer until the cold radiated over Sue's entire body. "Do tell. Details, kitten, details! The afterlife is so dull. The dead are dead, and the living never talk to me. Who's the bright spot?"

"Oh, uh..." Sue again looked at her chest but didn't see anything beyond the bedhead kitten. "I don't know what it is. I just met him. He gave me directions when my bus broke down. His name is Jameson Lloyd, and he owns the coffee shop."

"Not in town long enough for a booty call, huh?" Vivien teased under her breath with a playful shake of her head.

Julia turned to Vivien and demanded. "Is he worth ogling?"

"Oh, very much so." Vivien nodded, grinning. "Jameson Lloyd? Really? Score."

"Tell me," Julia said.

Sue opened her mouth, but she couldn't think of what to say.

"Nice. Charming. Modest. You never hear him

bragging about himself," Vivien supplied for her. "Everyone in school liked him from the jocks to the geeks. He never picked on Heather and me, and even defended us once."

"Good, good," Julia nodded. "What else?"

"Goes to church," Heather added, her words not as confident as if she tried to come up with details for her grandma. "Says nice things about his mother. Sponsors a little league team. Helps ladies with their groceries. Holds open doors for people. Um, I think someone mentioned he brought coffee and pastries and opened his house to people after those apart- ments caught fire years back."

Sue found herself smiling. Jameson did all that?

"Nice. Bring him by so I can see him, will you kitten?" Julia arched a brow and waited for Sue to nod. "That's a good kitten. Welcome to the club, Sue Jewel. Good luck. Hope you're around long enough to enjoy your new beau, but if not, I'll see you on the other side."

Julia started to fade.

"Grandma—ah, *Julia*, wait," Heather said.

Julia's translucent body returned; only her clothing changed from the pantsuit to a dress with small flowers. She looked older with fine lines around her eyes and a less aggressive smile.

"How can we help Sue?" Heather asked. "Her dead husband is coming after her."

"Not the first time, is it, kitten?" Julia asked Sue, though the question sounded rhetorical. Her voice was softer than before as if age had mellowed her. This version of Julia was less intimidating, somehow.

Sue shook her head. "No."

"We want to do a séance and banish him," Lorna said.

Julia frowned and shook her head. "No, that's a terrible idea. Don't do that."

"Earlier, you were saying something about smelling and seeing." Heather came to stand by Sue and placed a hand on her shoulder in support.

"I gave you the clues you need," Julia said.

"Please, Grandma, we need more." Heather went to the woman and lifted her hands to let them hover near her shoulders. "You told me that you sent us the rings and brought us together to help each other heal from our individual pains. Tell us how we help Sue. We don't need riddles. We need you to explain. The five senses, right? Smell, taste, sight, sound, touch. That's what you said earlier."

Julia nodded. "How far has it gotten?"

"Smell—" Heather started to answer.

Julia held up her hand to stop her. "Sue."

"Um," she glanced at Heather, who nodded at her in encouragement. "I smell his cologne and other things that remind me of him—gun oil, um, cigarettes. I taste his favorite liquor sometimes, instead of what I'm eating or drinking. It burns but I don't get drunk from it. That part has gotten better since I met these ladies."

Sue wished she sounded more confident but talking to a ghost was nerve-racking. The midnight coffee probably didn't help her anxiety either.

"The window," Lorna prompted.

"Tonight, I saw his face reflected behind me when I was trying to unlock the theater door," Sue said. "He didn't look well."

"Then I'm guessing he didn't die well," Julia said.

"Car accident. He was drunk and veered in front of a semi. It sent the car into a ravine." Sue glanced at the others and didn't say more.

"You should tell them," Vivien urged. "We're here to help."

"Um." A tear slipped down Sue's cheek, even as she tried to hold it back. "At the time, he had me wrapped in plastic in the trunk of the car."

Lorna gasped lightly and covered her mouth.

"Shit," Heather swore.

"Yeah," Vivien agreed with her.

"Julia, why can't we do a séance and send him on his way before things get worse?" Lorna asked. "That worked with others."

"You saw what rode in on Glenn's visit." Julia put her hands on her hips and frowned. "If you think summoning that demon with Lorna's cheating ex was bad, what exactly do you think is going to travel through the veil on the back of a wife-murdering anger ball like Sue's husband? You girls are going to need to start thinking these things through for yourself. I gave you my book. I've given you the rings. You have the tools and the magic. You're smart girls, but you need to use your noodles. I can't keep giving you the answers."

Sue swiped at her eyes.

*Demon?*

She couldn't ask the question.

Julia stared in her direction. Her form wavered like desert heat coming off a hot blacktop. Her voice sounded farther away. "Some things others can't do for you. Remember that. Inner strength does not come from outside. It can't be given."

In a blink, Julia disappeared. The light stopped flickering and shone brightly on the stage.

Sue looked around the seating area. "Where did she go?"

"She's said all she's going to say," Heather said. "The rest is up to us."

"It's late," Lorna said. "We need sleep if we're going to figure this all out."

Vivien went to the boxes of candy and handed them out. "Eat. You'll feel better after some sugar."

Sue followed their example and put a piece of chewy candy in her mouth, even though she didn't want to eat it. She was too shaken by what she'd seen.

"If it were me, I wouldn't want to be alone," Lorna said, picking the pillows up off the floor. "So, as long as Sue says yes, I'm voting slumber party."

Sue nodded, relieved not to be alone for the night.

"Good, come on," Heather took two of the pillows from Lorna and shuffled toward the stairs. "We'll hit this problem with fresh brains in the morning."

## CHAPTER NINE

How Sue could fall asleep after such a night, she would never know for sure. Perhaps it was because she felt so drained after the séance and sharing of emotions. Hank, Julia, ghosts, séances, rings, magic, demons—what the hell was she supposed to do with all that? Have a mental breakdown?

The night had started so... strange, beautiful, hopeful? With Jameson, she was able to forget herself. Such a sweet and simple thing to forget and be in a moment.

Lorna, Heather, and Vivien had shared the bed while Sue took the couch. She was grateful for her new friends, her *only* friends really. Even though she was tired when she woke, she couldn't fall back asleep and instead took a change of clothes down to the lobby to dress. She thought of Jameson and the store, wanting to see him and also wanting to do something nice for her friends. Lorna had brought her a few supplies the day before, but she didn't have any real groceries to serve everyone breakfast.

Sue stared at the window where she'd seen Hank's face, unable to force her hand to push the door open. She looked so hard her vision blurred the glass. Her heart beat a little too hard, *thump-thump-thumping* in her chest and throat and ears. She tried to breathe past the fear. Vivien had been right in her analogy. She was the scared horror movie teenager under the bed, watching the feet of her attacker in the moments before he grabbed her. It wasn't a matter of *if* the attack would come, but when.

"*Some things others can't do for you. Remember that.*"

Julia was right. She couldn't ask the others to face Hank. He was her demon. They didn't deserve to be dragged down with her.

"Okay, Hank," she whispered, "I'm here but leave them—"

Movement in the glass proceeded a firm knock. Sue gasped and jumped back in fright. A uniformed officer waved at her from the sidewalk.

It took Sue a moment to react. The man motioned down to the door handle before giving it a small shake to show it was locked.

Sue forced herself to calm as she reached to open the door.

The officer stepped inside. "Morning, ma'am, I'm Officer Hill. I'm looking for Sue Jewel. She around?"

Sue nodded. "That's me."

*Fucking Kathy.*

"We had a call this morning from St. Louis asking us to do a wellness check on you," Hill explained.

Sue forced a smile; it was an old habit to hide what she was feeling. "I'm well. Just here on a little vacation."

"Glad to hear it. Would you mind if I take a look at your license so that we can tell St. Louis we definitely talked to the right woman?"

Sue nodded and drew her purse around to her front to dig inside. She pulled out her wallet.

"How are you enjoying our town?" Hill asked.

"It's lovely," Sue said. "I'm actually thinking of staying."

*Shit, why did I say that? What if Hill tells the St. Louis cop who then tells Kathy?*

"Hm." He nodded.

Sue handed him her license. "I'm sorry this ended up being a thing. I guess someone was worried about me. I texted her last night, and it should all be cleared up by now."

"There seems to be some concern that you might do yourself harm," Hill said as he wrote down her license number. "If you're struggling, I can leave you the name of someone to talk to."

"Thank you, but I promise I'm fine. My mother-in-law tends to fall on the dramatic side. She just lost her son, my husband, and..." Sue's eyes went to the glass to search for Hank.

"I understand," Hill said. "But I'm going to leave you that number just in case. Better to have it if you need it than not."

"Thank you." Sue forced her gaze back to the man.

"Glad to see you're not in any danger, Mrs. Jewel. If that changes, be sure to give us a call. That's why we're here." Hill handed her the license and a business card for a counseling center. He gave her a kind smile. "Welcome to Freewild Cove. I'm sure I'll see you around."

Sue doubted the police would appreciate a call to investigate a ghost attack.

"Thank you."

The officer gave one last nod before pushing through the door. The cool morning breeze blew against her briefly as it shut. Her eyes followed the cop.

The door closed, and Hank's sunken face reflected where the man had been. Sue made a weak noise and covered her mouth to keep from screaming. Hank grinned at her, his smile too large for his face and his dark eyes filled with a familiar sickness. He disappeared as quickly as he appeared.

"Who were you talking to?" Lorna suppressed a yawn as she moved to join her. She still wore her pajama pants. "Did someone try to show up early for their booking?"

"No, it's nothing," Sue dismissed.

Lorna went to the door and leaned into it, close to where Hank Had been. Sue gasped and started to reach out to stop her, but Lorna pulled away.

"Police?" Lorna asked in surprise. "What did they want?"

"My mother-in-law called them when she couldn't find me," Sue said. "I forgot to call and ask her permission before running out of my haunted house."

Lorna frowned. "So she called the cops? That's a little controlling, isn't it?"

Sue shrugged. She kept an eye on the door to make sure Hank stayed out of the reflection. Maybe if she smashed the spirit glass she could get rid of him? How mad would Heather be? The twenty-thousand-dollar check in her purse would cover the damage.

"Sue?" Lorna touched her arm, jolting her out of her thoughts.

"The cop needed to make sure I wasn't a danger to myself," Sue said. "Kathy told them I was suicidal."

"What?" Lorna frowned in annoyance. "You're not suicidal."

"No, I'm not. She also told them I am addicted to pain killers." Sue looked at her hands, unable to meet the woman's eyes.

Lorna ran her hand down Sue's arm to take her hand. "That's what that was."

"What?" Sue stiffened. At the touch, her hair began to lift with a static charge, and she felt Lorna's concern flowing into her.

"That need to be numb. Vivien felt it too when I healed you that first night. That gnawing, desperate need." A tear slipped down Lorna's face. "The pleasure of being wrapped in the dull warmth of unfeeling bliss."

Sue pulled her hand away. "I'm not addicted."

Lorna tried to smile, but the look was strained with pity.

"But I could have been. I felt the pull, the charm of being lost, of turning off the pain, of forgetting as my mind faded into the white noise of a land where nothing mattered." Sue ran her hand along her ribs. "I had resisted for years, but the night of my accident, they put something in my IV. I thought I was dying in that trunk, and then I woke up numb in the hospital. I didn't want my ribs to heal because I didn't want the excuse to be sedated to go away. I wanted to drift in the white noise forever. Eventually, the bruises went away, the funeral was long over, and I had no more excuses. Hank's smell had started appearing. The doctors said my head injury could cause side effects. So I flushed the pills."

"Good." Lorna nodded.

"I'm not addicted, but I could be, and I acknowledge that I have that weakness in me." Sue ran her hands through her hair and took a deep breath. She looked around the quiet lobby, automatically wondering if ghosts watched them even now.

"I can only begin to guess what you've been through, but I can see the appeal of escape. Be proud of yourself for resisting." Lorna made a move to touch her again, but Sue stepped back.

"The same day I flushed the pills, the smells became stronger." Sue frowned in realization. "It's like when I was numb, I could ignore it, but when I was clear, I let it all in. That's the night everything started tasting like bourbon, and my television became possessed with messages to come to Freewild Cove."

Lorna walked closer to the glass touching the surface before stepping back.

"Do you think Hank is trying to get me to...?" Sue rubbed her temples.

"Drive you to kill yourself by overdose?" Lorna finished. "We're not going to let that happen."

"I don't think that's what he wants." Sue stared at the glass door, willing it to shatter with her mind. "That seems a little passive for Hank's tastes. He's always been more of a hands-on doer."

The ring sent pulses of energy through Sue's body.

"Sue—" Lorna barely got the word out when suddenly the door shattered with a loud *pop!*

Lorna jerked Sue's arm, pulling her out of the way as shards of glass sprinkled onto the ground.

The sound of footsteps came stampeding down the stairs from the apartment.

"Did you see what happened?" Lorna asked. "Did someone throw a rock?"

"I'm sorry," Sue whispered, tugging at the ring still pulsing on her hand. "I didn't mean to."

"What was that?" Vivien appeared with Heather, and they both began examining the door.

Sue wasn't sure how she did it, but it felt clear that she had. She willed the mess to rewind like it never happened. Heather had been so kind. She didn't deserve Sue wrecking her property.

Heather sighed and crossed her arms over her chest. Then, with a tone that revealed she was determined to fix things, she said, "All right. I'll get a broom and start cleaning this up. We'll need plastic sheeting. What time is it? I need to call my supplier. I hope they can get us a door today before—"

The broken glass began to clink softly as if shaking. They all stopped to stare.

"Earthquake?" Vivien whispered. "Here?"

The glass shards leaped up from the ground, fitting together like a million tiny puzzle pieces as the door rebuilt itself. When every last piece had fallen into place, the three women turned to look at her. First, they stared at her face and then, one by one, moved their attention to where she tugged on the ring.

"How did you?" Heather moved to test the door, pushing it open and letting it fall shut. "It's as good as new."

"Did anyone see?" Lorna joined Heather at the door and peered out.

"I didn't mean to break it," Sue said.

"I don't think anyone noticed," Lorna said. "Thank goodness. I'm not sure how we'd explain what happened."

"I was upset and..." She wasn't sure how to rationalize her willing something into action with her mind.

"You cleaned up the mess," Lorna finished with a grin.

"You're a cleaner," Vivien exclaimed. She hurried behind the concessions counter and grabbed a box of candy from the display. Opening it, she flung her hand and sent candy scattering across the floor. Some of it pelted Heather on the legs.

"Hey, watch it," Heather grumbled.

Sue looked at the mess Vivien had made.

Vivien set the empty candy box on the counter. "All right let's see what you can do. Clean it up."

Sue began to reach for the candy on the floor to pick it up.

"No, not like that. With your magic," Vivien instructed.

Sue's ring had stopped pulsing. "I don't know how."

"Focus," Lorna said. "Think about what you want."

Heather crossed her arms over her chest, and she stayed quiet as she watched.

"I want..." Sue lifted her hand helplessly to the side. "I want the candy back in the box?"

The candy remained on the floor.

"With conviction," Vivien urged. "Try again."

Sue took a deep breath and stared at the floor, wanting it to be clean. A giant jolt of electricity shot up her arm from the ring and seemed to explode out of her. The candy began to tremble and shake just as the glass shards had. The colorful pieces flew into the air, spinning like a tornado before arching to rain into the box in loud thuds. Before the last thud had even sounded, dust floated from the floor. Though the floor hadn't looked dirty, the tiny particles created their own cyclone and spun around the lobby. It accumulated dust from the concessions, from the restroom signs, and molding on the high ceilings. It even pulled a piece of stale popcorn from underneath.

The dust storm slashed between Heather and Lorna, sending their hair flying. Lorna cried out and blocked her face with her arms.

"Sue!" Heather yelled. "That's enough."

"I don't know how to stop it!" Sue didn't understand how she'd started it. How could she end it?

The dust flew at the door, crashing into the glass. It rippled like desert sand, folding over itself before pushing into the seam along the door's edge to blow away into the breeze outside. When the last speck of dirt disappeared, a single kernel of popcorn remained. It didn't fit through the crack, and after hovering for a few seconds, it fell and bounced to a stop on the floor.

Heather slowly walked over to the popcorn and picked it up. She examined it before carrying it to a trash can near the concessions and dropped it inside. "Okay, then. You're a cleaner."

Sue bit the inside of her lip.

"What?" Lorna asked. "That doesn't make you happy?"

"I've spent my adult life making sure Hank's house was just as he wanted it." Sue gave a dejected shrug. "I find it sad that my magical power is cleaning."

"Our gifts aren't always what we want, but what we know how to do," Vivien said. "Lorna's a healer and finder because that's who she's been her whole life. She takes care of others. I'd rather not be in people's heads all the time, and I know Heather would love not to have ghosts yelling in her ear for attention when she's talking to people."

"True that." Heather looked around the lobby. She ran her finger over several surfaces. "You did a damn good job."

"I wouldn't look at it as a disappointing thing." Lorna crouched down to look at the floor. "I'd think of it as you spent so much time cleaning, you don't have to do it anymore. It's a reward for time served." She gave a low whistle. "Wow, these floors look brand new out of the factory. Even the grimy rubbery smudge is gone. I've been scrubbing at that thing for months."

"I need some air." Sue looked at the door, nervous about going through it to the other side.

"Air or coffee?" Vivien nudged her arm. "I could go for coffee."

"You're in pajamas," Heather pointed out.

"Sue's not." Vivien grinned. "Sue can pick up coffees for us. Can't you, Sue?"

Sue felt her cheeks turning red.

"Oh, please, Sue, please," Lorna begged.

Vivien gave a meaningful look at Heather, who quickly added, "Oh, yeah, I could sure use a coffee. And by coffee, I mean a vanilla latte with an extra shot of espresso."

"Same," Vivien said.

"Same for me too. I'll get you cash," Lorna offered, moving toward the back office.

"No, this is on me. It's the least I can do." Sue didn't feel like she had much of a choice and finally forced herself to go outside. She glanced back as the door closed, but instead of Hank's reflection, she saw Vivien smiling at her. The woman gave her a thumbs up and waved at her to go.

# CHAPTER TEN

SUE INTENTIONALLY DID NOT LOOK into reflective surfaces as she walked down the sidewalk toward the coffee shop. Instead, she focused on her steps and her breathing.

*In. Out. In. Out.*

Jameson already told her Stu covered the coffee shop in the morning, so she didn't expect to see him there. She opened her purse as she walked and pulled out the loyalty card for the free latte and ran her finger over his signature on the back. Remembering their night together doing inventory, she smiled.

Someone bumped into Sue's arm, catching her attention.

"Oh, sorry," a woman said with a laugh, holding up her cell phone. "I wasn't paying attention."

Sue smiled and started to answer, but realized the woman was in the middle of a video chat and hadn't been apologizing to her.

"I know what you're doing," the woman said to the phone screen. "Don't think I don't."

Sue ignored the woman and put the card back in her purse. As silly as it might seem, she wasn't going to redeem it. She turned the corner, and her eyes automatically searched for the coffee shop entrance. She quickened her pace. A large group walked in before she could reach it. She slowed her step.

*Tap. Tap. Tap.*

Sue glanced down at the sound. Ace the cat stared up at her, pawing the window as if to get her attention. His fluffy white body was settled between a book on finding inner peace and a romance novel. The long fur seemed to swallow the edges of the covers. His mouth opened, and she heard the faintest meow.

Sue didn't think as she went into the bookstore. A tiny bell dinged overhead. Ace appeared in front of her and looked back. The second she reached out to pet him, he started walking away. He went several feet before glancing around as if to make sure she followed him.

"Aren't you the little rascal?" Sue whispered. The old wooden floorboards squeaked as she walked on them. "Playing hard to get."

Ace led her to a hollow square-shaped sales counter in the middle of the shop and disappeared behind it, knocking open a café swinging door with his body. She peeked over the side but didn't follow the cat in.

Sue turned to study the bookshop. On each side of the sales counter were two different sections. To the right stood a small stage with chairs around it. She assumed for visiting authors. To the left, more books were stacked neatly on the taller shelves. Handwritten labels separated them by category. Author quotes were painted in fine script on the walls, so tiny she had to lean close to read them. Old paperbacks were stacked to create unique patterns with their worn pages and cracked spines on a shelf toward the very back marked, *"Well Loved."*

She liked that, *well loved*. It was so much better than, *used* or *old* or *discarded*.

It occurred to her that as people aged and became worn and cracked, they should be able to say they were well loved. Not discarded. Not old. Not useless or used or past a prime.

A tear slipped down her cheek.

Not thrown into a trunk on their fortieth birthday because their worth was over, because all that was left was age on a once youthful face and extra padding on hips.

It was a memory she had tucked away into the deep recesses of her mind because it was too painful to relive. Hank didn't try to kill her because she'd done something wrong, or because she was a crappy housewife, but because he knew that she would get old like any other human, and he could not have his image tarnished by her wrinkles.

"Meh," Ace loudly protested her line of thought from somewhere behind the counter, drawing her out of the memory so she could lock the door on it once more.

Sue gave a small laugh and said under her breath, "Meh, is right, buddy."

There was something safe and charming to small independent bookstores. The most notable being that there were no televisions for ghosts or magic to possess. Bookstores were so innocent looking, so warm and welcoming, like a giant hug waiting to invite you in. And yet, they were filled with every imaginable adventure known to man. Spotting an alien romance cover, she chuckled and corrected—known to man or extraterrestrial.

The wealth of human experience could be read in books. Here those alien romances mingled with highbrow literature, both equal but with different purposes—one to inform, the other to entertain. Classics danced with nonfiction. They all waited for someone to pick them up and lay them open, to explore everything they had to offer.

What kind of person ended up owning a place like this? In a town like Freewild Cove? Next to a coffee shop with Jameson as an owner?

What did she want?

Who could she be?

Could she be this?

Her hand tingled, a sign she now knew to heed. The dream became quietly clear. She wanted honest, thoughtful work. She was meant to be here, in this place. When she followed Ace inside, she had expected to pet him, maybe browse as she waited for the large group to get their coffees. Instead, she had been struck unexpectedly with something more. She turned a slow circle, looking around as the image of a future dared to become apparent.

The bookshop owner and the coffee shop owner.

What went together better than books and coffee? Or tea, of course?

She and Jameson?

Sue smiled as she drew a finger along a row of spines. She used to love falling into a book, reading until the sun peeked through her window. Even in the drowsy aftermath, she didn't resent the exhaustion as the words stayed with her and carried her through. It has been such a simple pleasure, one she hadn't indulged in years. When life became about survival, simple pleasures were the first to go.

Sue found a small reading nook buried between the ends of two shelves. A young boy had taken up occupancy there, curling up with a book that looked much older than his reading level, if the scary clown on the cover was any indication. Even so, he was enthralled and didn't notice her walk past.

Sue paused when she was mostly out of his eyesight and leaned to watch him for a moment. Suddenly, he turned to look at her. "You think I don't know what's in that head of yours?"

Sue stiffened. "What did you say?"

The boy blinked. "I didn't say anything."

He turned back to his book, his attention disappearing inside the pages.

"Oh, ah, sorry." Sue retraced her steps.

Ace sat on the sales counter, licking his paw. Sue lifted her hand to pet him now that he was finally still and in range. His head moved to butt her palm as if welcoming her greeting.

Sue smiled at the animal as it soaked up her attention. "Thank you for showing me your place. You're fortunate to get to live here."

A bustle of energy in the form of a short woman appeared from the side of the store that had the stage. Cat-eye-shaped glasses and bright lipstick offset black hair streaked with gray piled into a bun on her head. She looked like a character from a book, though Sue couldn't determine precisely which book.

The woman stopped and looked at Sue in surprise, then to where Sue petted Ace. The cat jumped off the counter and rushed toward the well-loved books. Papers fluttered behind him, knocked to the floor. Sue saw the boy's hand drop from the chair to absently pet the cat, even as the rest of him was hidden by the shelves.

"I'll get these." Sue instantly leaned down to pick up the papers.

The woman came to lean on the counter to watch. "Do you believe in signs?"

"Signs?" Sue glanced at the woman before

tapping the papers on the floor to align them in a pile. She slowly stood and placed them on the counter.

"I do," the woman said.

"I..." Sue glanced around in confusion, looking for a sign on the walls that she might have disobeyed. "Was I not supposed to pet Ace?"

The woman frowned. "Why wouldn't you pet Ace?"

"I..." Sue frowned. "I'm confused. What sign?"

"What's your name, love?"

"Sue, ah, Susan Jewel."

"Nice to meet you, Sue. I'm Melba." The woman put her hand on the stack of papers Sue had picked up for her. Each motion seemed to tremble with an energetic force. "I'm talking about cosmic signs. When the universe whispers and you're lucky enough to hear it."

Sue leaned forward to whisper, "You mean magical powers?"

Just how unique was this town? Did everyone have secret magical powers?

Melba chuckled. "I wish magic. How cool would that be! Though, I suppose there is a kind of everyday magic in things that happen to us."

Sue couldn't help but return the smile. "All right. So what is the cosmic sign?"

"You're meant to be here," Melba stated, as if it was an obvious fact. "Ace is never wrong in his judgment of people."

Sue looked around. "It is a great store."

"I know," Melba nodded.

"Ace is a fantastic cat," Sue added.

"He's a naughty scamp," Melba said with a shrug. "But I love him. He's never wrong."

"So you said." Sue felt the natural end of a conversation coming and started to pull away.

"Ten thousand," Melba said.

"Ten thousand what?" Sue stopped her slow departure.

Melba tapped her fingernail on the stack of papers. "To buy out my business. It includes all the inventory, contacts, etcetera, etcetera. Not the building. We lease."

Sue glanced down and read the page heading, "*The Bookstore in Freewild Cove Sales Contract Page Five of Seven.*"

"Cosmic, right?"

"Uh," Sue glanced around. "I think maybe you were expecting someone else?"

"No." Melba shook her head. "I'm pretty sure it's you. Ace is never wrong. I've had these contracts sitting here for roughly four months. I woke up one

177

night and had a feeling right here." She pushed her fist to the center of her chest. "It's time for the last chapter of my business owner book and I should be moving into the epilogue soon. I knew that the right person would find this contract. Not a single person has touched them since I put them here, and don't let today's lack of foot traffic fool you. A lot of people have come in."

"But why would you want to sell? This place is amazing?" Nerves balled in Sue's stomach. Just minutes ago, she had been daydreaming about a different life.

"It is, isn't it? And I couldn't just sell to anyone. I need to know that the universe approves." Melba slapped her hands on the counter a few times and then propelled herself back a few steps. "But I'm turning sixty years young soon, and there are things I want to do."

"You don't look sixty," Sue said.

"That's good because I won't be for another five years," Melba answered.

Five years was soon?

"What is it you want to do?" Sue asked.

"Not bother with business taxes while I sit back and collect a paycheck." Melba grinned. "That's the catch. I come with the store—as an employee, of course. I figure three years is more than enough time to show someone the ropes. That way, I know I'm leaving it in good hands. Now, I won't lie. It's not easy being a small business owner. It's not just selling hard copies anymore. We have to have an online presence with e-books and a portal for customers to order books they want, and we do a book fair at the local schools every year. They don't make a lot of money, but kids need books."

"Melba, this is so..." Sue felt her hand tingle.

"Also, you'll be expected to read to Ace. He likes it when you perform scenes from some of the books." Melba nodded emphatically. "He's a naughty bugger. Loves vampire romances."

"Oh?" Sue tried not to laugh. "I don't know if—"

"Is it the ten thousand? That's more of a rough estimate. We can run an inventory report—"

"No, ten thousand seems very fair, if not *too* cheap for a place like this," Sue interrupted. "I..."

She thought of the check in her purse. Could she do this?

The ring sent a pulse through her hand so powerful that she gasped and had to grab her palm. "Ow."

"What is it?" Melba hurried through the café doors to come around the counter next to Sue.

"Nothing. Hand stinger." Sue flicked her hand several times to shake off the sensation.

"I hate those." Melba leaned against the counter.

This was insanity even to consider. She had a house in St. Louis.

A house she hated with memories she hated even more, close to a mother-in-law who told people she was a suicidal opiate addict who had been a burden on her perfect son.

She had... what? What did she have besides those things?

Nothing. She had nothing. There was no life back in St. Louis. Here she had new friends, a budding affection for Jameson. Who knew where that would lead, but wasn't it worth finding out? She looked at her hand. She had Julia's magic. Lorna was right. Something was appealing about never having to clean.

Then again, all of this might not matter. If Hank's spirit came for her, if these were her last moments, where did she want to spend them?

The answer was easy. Sue swallowed nervously. She felt a warm brush against her legs and looked down to see Ace rubbing against her.

"I can pay cash," Sue said. The second the words were out, she felt warmth flooding her body and knew this was the decision she was supposed to make. "I'll need to deposit a check, maybe open a bank account here, so I'm not sure how much time that will take for it to clear a new account."

"Handshake deal works for me." Melba slid the papers a few inches away from them, more as a symbolic gesture. "The details can wait."

"I might need a little time to figure some things out." Sue took Melba's offered hand and shook it.

"Take your time. Ace and I will be here waiting." Melba whistled and leaned down to pick Ace up from the floor. She scratched his head as she carried him around the sales counter toward the stage. "Did you hear that? You have a new lady to protect."

Sue followed, watching Melba move toward a door labeled, "*Queen of the Books.*"

She looked at the store in wonder. Would this place be hers?

A tiny thread of panic tried to unravel from a place of doubt. It wasn't too late. There had only been a handshake. She could change her mind.

Muffled noise drew her attention to the sidewalk outside. The large group that beat her to the coffee line had begun to conjugate there. Sue left the book-store and stood in the doorway, partly in shock, partly in excitement.

What did she want?

What had she just done?

Was this who she was now? An impulsive book-store owner in Freewild Cove?

Suddenly, she smiled.

Yes. That was who she was now. And it felt right.

## CHAPTER ELEVEN

THE SMELL of brewing coffee made her smile. Soft classic rock came over the speakers, underscoring the low murmur of customers' voices. Almost everyone sat down at tables, not paying her any attention. She looked for Jameson but didn't see him.

"Laney," a man announced from behind the counter. He had pulled his long hair into a man-bun.

Sue hid her smile, knowing that it must be Stu.

A twenty-something sauntered up to the counter and began flirting for her coffee. Sue glanced up at the menu board and pretended to read it. She was the only person in line, and there was no reason to interrupt the youthful interaction.

"Yo, what can I get you?" Stu approached, pulling a pencil from behind his ear. He began tapping it along with the music and sang a few heart-felt bars.

"Four vanilla lattes with an extra shot to go," she ordered.

"Fine choice. You are looking to ride a caffeine buzz. Cool. Cool." Stu didn't write it down but continued drumming his pencil in the air as he bobbed his head in time to the music. He turned to make her coffees.

"Hey, is your boss in by chance?" Sue asked. "Jameson?"

"Yeah," Stu said as if surprised. "Dude's never here this early on the slow days. I don't know what's up with that. He keeps popping his head out of the office and checking on me. Like I'm going to run off with the coffeemaker."

Sue hadn't expected him to say yes. She inhaled deeply and held her breath.

"Wait." Stu stopped making her lattes and grinned. "You're here for Jameson?"

Sue gave a weak nod.

Stu's grin widened. "Damn, the boss has some game after all. It's about time he macked on some honeys."

Sue laughed at his obvious good humor. "I don't

think anyone has ever called me a honey. Or said I was macked on."

Stu winked at her and started dancing his way back to the lattes. "Maybe not to your face, lady-lady."

Sue couldn't help smiling. Suddenly, everything Jameson hinted at with Stu made sense. This young man was clearly a handful, and his good mood was infectious.

"I'll come back for those," Sue said.

Stu waved a hand to indicate he heard her.

Sue went to the office door and lightly knocked.

"It's open!" Jameson yelled.

Sue opened the door and peeked in. Nervous pleasure unfurled inside her. "Just stopping by to say hello."

"Hey, it's my favorite new employee," Jameson announced from his desk with a friendly wave. "Come in!"

"You might not want to let Stu hear you say that." Sue stood in the doorway.

"I did say *new*." Jameson stood and came around the desk. He reached to close the door behind her, so they were alone. "But perhaps you're right. I don't want to hurt his feelings. He made it in on time this morning."

Jameson didn't return to his seat as he remained standing with her.

"I have some bad news," Sue said. "I have to turn in my two weeks' notice."

His smile fell. "You're leaving town?"

She leaned against the office door. The solid boundary helped her stay upright as he neared. Something about him made her stomach flip-flop and her knees weak. What the hell was this teenage-nonsense-reaction all about?

"Actually, it looks like I might be staying," Sue said.

His smile instantly returned. "Really? What decided it for you? Was it the free latte?"

Sue nodded and joked, "That was one of the deciding factors, yes."

"Always is."

Sue laughed. The conversation flowed so easily with him.

"Wait, if you're moving to town, doesn't that mean you'll need a job? Are you sure you want to give up the coveted position of barista so hastily?" Jameson managed a somber expression.

"Well, if it's coveted..."

"Oh, it is." He assured her.

"If my new endeavor doesn't work out, I might be

back begging for the position," Sue said. "Hopefully, you'll put a good notation in my employee file so I can come back."

"Hm, I suppose I can put in there that you're a good counter," he said. "I know for a fact you can make it all the way up to sixty-seven."

"Sixty-nine candles," she corrected.

"Huh, I should fix that. I guess I couldn't read my own writing from last night." Jameson went to the desk and grabbed a sticky note. As he wrote, he said, "sixty-nine candles," and circled it several times.

"That was a close call. It's a good thing I stopped by or your paperwork would have been wrong." Sue pushed away from the door now that he was farther away from her.

Jameson sat on the edge of his desk and crossed his arms over his chest. "So, did you just stop by to leave me understaffed?"

"And to say hi."

"Hi." He dropped his arms to his sides and rested his hands on the edge of the desk.

"Hi." Sue tried not to blush, but she felt her cheek flushing slightly at his attention. "Last night you said you own the bookstore building, right?"

"I do." He nodded.

"I guess that means you're going to be my new landlord." Sue watched his face closely for a reaction.

"Are you moving from the theater into the bookstore? If so, when you get tired of books, I have a cot in back you can use if you want to continue your business-hopping trend."

"I'm buying the bookstore from Melba. There are still some details to iron out, but, yeah, we agreed." Sue didn't take her eyes from him.

He stared at her as if waiting for a punchline. When she didn't say anything more, he asked, "Are you serious?"

Sue nodded.

"But you didn't even know there was a bookstore until last night. Unless I misunderstood?" The light-hearted mood changed somewhat.

"I don't know. Ace lured me in again today. I saw how great the store was, and Melba came out, and we started talking about cosmic signs, and there were contracts and... it made sense." Sue looked at the floor. Now that I've said that out loud, it does sound a little sudden, doesn't it?"

"I don't know. I mean, if Melba was seeing her cosmic signs." Jameson scratched the back of his head.

"Are you upset? Do you not want me as a tenant?

I can pay a deposit." Sue had no idea how much the rent was, but evidently, the store could afford to pay it since it was still in business. "I'm quiet, clean, and I swear I won't be any trouble."

"No, I don't want you as a renter," he confessed.

Sue tried to answer but didn't know what to say to that. "Oh."

"I wanted to ask you out on a date, but if I'm your landlord, that makes me a creeper."

He did?

Sue couldn't help her relieved smile. "We haven't signed anything yet. We just agreed to agree. So technically, you're not my landlord. Yet."

"Good to know." He nodded slowly.

"So...?"

"So what?" He arched a brow.

"Are you going to ask me out?"

"Depends. Are you going to say yes if I do?"

Sue nodded.

"How about..." Jameson looked at the clock on the wall. "Now?"

Sue laughed. "Now?"

"I like you. It's not often I meet a woman who can," he smirked as if catching himself and finished with, "count."

"If women around here can't count, then I'd say

the first order of business is to overhaul the school system."

"So, now?" he persisted. "I don't want to give you a chance to change your mind."

"Tonight and I promise I won't change my mind?"

He pushed up from the desk and stepped closer to her. "I'll pick you up at the theater at eight."

Sue nodded, not backing away. She automatically glanced at his mouth. Her voice was breathy as she answered, "Eight."

"Eight," he repeated, leaning a little closer. His breath fanned her lips.

"Eight." Sue licked her lips in anticipation.

"Okay."

"Okay."

Jameson leaned in slowly, giving her time to back out. Sue didn't think, just acted. She pressed her mouth to his.

His kiss started gently as if asking permission rather than taking. She leaned into him, her hands lifting to rest on his chest. He caressed her arms before reaching around her back to bring her closer.

With each second, the kiss intensified. Sue didn't want to stop and think. Her body felt starved for affection, and here he was offering it to her freely.

The closer they inched together, the more erotic the movements felt. Every tiny shift sent awareness humming through her. His unmistakable interest bumped into her, and he suddenly pulled away.

"I'm sorry," he managed, breathing hard. "I didn't mean to get carried away."

Sue wanted him to come back. There was no denying how she felt. Grandma Julia had been right when she read Sue's aura. There was a bright spot in Sue's chest now, and it had a lot to do with meeting Jameson. She needed that light to grow, not fade. A warning whispered in the back of her mind. If Hank came for her, at least she wouldn't regret not taking this moment.

"I'm not sorry you did that." Sue went to him, reaching to pull his face back to hers. She resumed kissing him, letting her body press against him fully.

Jameson moaned in surprise. He walked toward her, reaching his arm behind her. The motion was a little awkward, but as she heard the office door lock, she realized what he was doing.

"Are you sure because I don't want you to feel pressured?" He kept his voice quiet as he glanced at the office door.

Sue reached for his belt buckle. Excitement pumped through her. "I'm sure."

Jameson kissed her, deeper this time. His tongue slid past her lips, changing from gentle to passionate. She managed to get his belt unbuckled.

"This is crazy," he said against her mouth in between kisses. "I never do things like this."

"That's my line," she answered.

Images flashed through her mind as if doubts tried to worm their way in. She thought of the car trunk, of waking up in the hospital with a second chance to live. She wanted that chance. She wanted to live.

Jameson pulled back. "I'm serious. I don't do things like this."

Sue breathed hard. "Do you want to stop?"

"Hell, no." He took a step toward her, walking her back until she bumped up against the desk. He leaned his forehead to hers. "But I don't want you to think this is a thing I do with just anyone."

"I don't do this either, but I like you. I can't explain why. I just feel it, and I need to feel something good. I *want* to feel something good." She caressed his face. "I think I spent so much time hesitant and scared. I'm done with that. I want to be here, now, with you."

"Okay," he whispered.

Sue smiled. "Okay."

She reached for her jeans and unfastened them before pushing them from her hips. She used her toes to pull out of her shoes before kicking the jeans from her legs.

Jameson began to lean into her. He stopped. "Don't move."

Jameson rushed around the desk to dig inside a drawer before shoving it closed and looking in another. He pulled out a smashed box of condoms and examined the sides.

"Not expired," he said in relief, taking one out of the box as he came back around the desk to rejoin her. He dropped the box on the desk. A light murmur of voices rose from the coffee shop, and they both glanced at the door. When it settled back down, he asked, "Where were we?"

Sue laughed and resumed kissing him. There was no more hesitance or questioning as passion overtook everything else.

Jameson lifted her onto the desktop. Papers fluttered to the floor like in a scene from a movie. Her legs hung over the side.

Jameson unzipped his jeans and pushed them down, so they clung to his thighs. He put the condom on before coming to her. That first intimate brush caused a sharp gasp to escape her, and she bit her lip to try to stay quiet.

Sue had never experienced anything like being with Jameson. He kept his eyes open, gazing into her with a look of wonder as if he couldn't believe she was with him. The ring on her hand tingled, and she began to feel him inside her—not just his body but his soul. She had detected his kind heart, but now she felt it beating in time with hers. This was a good and caring man. He could no more hurt a woman than he could stop breathing.

"What is that?" he whispered in awe.

"Magic," she breathed into his ear, rocking her hips into him.

She fell back on the desk, bracing herself as the rhythm became frenzied. When Sue met her release, she felt her entire body explode with the pleasure of it. Jameson met his release seconds after her.

Breathing hard, he braced his hand on the desk next to her. They took a moment to recover. After some time, he straightened and turned away from her. He dropped the condom in the trash can and righted his clothing.

Sue hopped down from the desk and redressed.

When she finished, he pulled her into his arms

and held her. "I don't know if you felt it too, but that was..."

"Amazing," she finished for him.

"Magical," he said.

"Perfect."

"Magical."

"Wonderful."

"Magical."

Sue laughed. "I think you said that already."

He grinned. "Hey, you got to give a guy a break. I can barely think straight right now. You're lucky I'm speaking English."

Sue stroked his hair away from his forehead. "I have to say I'm thrilled you're not my landlord yet."

"If this was your way of negotiating a discount on rent, consider the building free." Jameson chuckled and cupped her face. "Where did you come from, Susan Sue?"

"St. Louis."

"Are you sure you're not an angel?" Jameson laughed and shook his head. "Sorry, that sounds like a bad line now that I've said it."

"It was kinda, yeah," Sue teased.

He kissed her softly. "How did I get so lucky? The odds of me stopping to get gas that late at night, at a station I never go to, at the exact same time your bus breaks down, have to be astronomical. Then for you to stay down the block and happen to be walking on the rare night I'm here late doing inventory. It feels like something bigger has a hand in this."

"What if I told you magic is real?"

"I'll believe anything you tell me." His expression changed, and he turned serious. "You said something earlier about being scared."

"Did I?" She averted her gaze.

"You said you needed to feel something good, but the way you said it was like you hadn't had much good. Then you said you spent too much time being hesitant and scared."

Sue stroked his cheek. "You listened when I said that."

Jameson ran his thumb over her lips. "Of course I did. I listen to everything you say."

"No, I mean, you really listened to me."

"Sue, I don't know if you realize this, but regardless of the length of time I've known you, I'm really into you. It's not because we had sex. I wasn't expecting that to happen, at least not without buying you several dinners first. *Not* that I'm complaining. I haven't been able to stop thinking about you since the gas station. You looked so tired and sad and even a little terrified. I wanted to hug you. Then last night, just hanging out here counting inventory, I've not enjoyed myself like that in a long time."

"I feel the same. I enjoy being with you, too."

Jameson's eyes implored her. "What's been scaring you? Talk to me. Are you hiding from someone? Is that why you looked frightened at the gas station? If you're in trouble, I'll help you."

At that, she kissed him on the corner of his mouth. "There's nothing you can do but thank you for caring."

"Are you scared now?"

She shook her head. "No. Here with you, I'm not scared."

"Talk to me, Sue. What's going on?"

Sue took a deep breath and stepped away from him. She pushed strands of loose hair back from her face. Maybe it was like pulling off a bandage. She just needed to tell him. "I turned forty four months ago."

"I don't care about age," he said.

"On my birthday, my husband decided I was too old and that he didn't want to be married anymore." Sue looked at the floor and took a steadying breath.

"So you're married? Separated? Divorced?" Jameson asked. "I can't imagine any man letting you go. If you need time, just say the word and we can take this as slow as you—"

Sue held up her hand to quiet him. She knew he wanted to understand her, but it took her a moment to form the words. "He hit me. Often. And never where anyone could see the damage."

Jameson stiffened, his expression darkening.

"On my birthday, he hit me with a hammer, wrapped me in plastic sheeting, and stuffed me in the trunk of our car." Her hands began to shake. "By all rights, I should be dead, but Hank crashed into a semi on the way to dump my body. I was thrown out of the trunk. Hank was killed. I woke up in a hospital. They told me he was drunk driving. A detective suspected that something was off, but she had no proof. Hank went down as a tragic accident, and no one knows what happened in our marriage but me. And no one in St. Louis who knew us would believe me if I told them. He was a lawyer, which I guess naturally made him a great liar. He once told me that when it comes down to brass tacks all that matters is who can make the most persuasive argument, not the truth. Hank was compelling. The secret shame of our marriage died with him."

"Sue..." Jameson offered his hand to her.

Sue didn't take it. If he held her, she wouldn't be

able to finish telling him. "The worst part is when it happened, I wasn't even surprised. There was a part of me that knew it would end that way."

"Sue." His tone became more insistent.

"The short of the relationship is, he drank, he hit me, I tried to leave and he always found me. I had nowhere to go, no money of my own, and being a lawyer, he had friends in the police department. I didn't love him, not after the first year of marriage. I prayed for an out." Sue gave a tiny shake of her entire body as if that could make the feelings go away. "So there you have it."

"That's not right," Jameson said. "No one deserves to be treated like that."

"I know." Sue held her hand out for him to take. "But I'm not living in the past. I'm here, now, with you."

Sue couldn't bring herself to say she was being haunted. Dumping one baggage bomb on him was enough.

"Besides." She drew him closer. "Why would I want to think about that when I have magic in front of me?"

Jameson wanted to say more. She saw the emotions in his eyes. Instead, he cupped her face and kissed her. "Yes, magic."

Sue wanted the lightness back in their conversation. The ring on her hand tingled its magic up her arm. She felt the connection between them building. His nearness steadied her and made her feel safe.

"You are the most amazing woman I've ever met," he said. "I wish I could explain what I feel. It's like..."

"What if I told you I think you feel magic? Real magic?" She took a deep breath. "That I was drawn to Freewild Cove by that same magic."

"I'll believe anything you tell me." He said it, but clearly, he didn't understand what she was telling him.

"Promise not to freak out." Sue concentrated on the papers scattered on the floor.

Jameson turned to follow her gaze. "What is it?"

Her hand tingled as she willed the papers back onto the desk. They began to flutter. Suddenly, the papers swept up from the floor and landed on the desk in a neat pile.

Jameson stared at the desk, then at her, and then back again. "How...?"

Sue instantly regretted the impulsive decision. Maybe it was too much, too soon.

No. She didn't want a life with secrets and lies, not anymore. She was who she was. He would have to decide for himself if he wanted a ticket on her crazy train.

"Did you...?" He stepped away from her.

"Now you know all my secrets, Jameson." Sue picked her purse up from the floor and reached for the doorknob. "I hope it hasn't scared you away, but if you don't come tonight for our date, I'll understand. Please excuse me. Lorna, Vivien, and Heather are waiting for me to bring back vanilla lattes."

"Eight o'clock," he said after her as she stepped out of the office.

Sue smiled at the door as it closed between them.

# CHAPTER TWELVE

"Where the hell did you go for coffee? The Amazon jungle?" Vivien demanded, moving to take the lattes from Sue when she stepped into the theater lobby. Without waiting for an answer, she yelled, "Lattes are here!"

"Where are the others?" Sue held a bag of muffins clutched in a fist.

"Lorna is in the office returning calls, and Heather is upstairs taking a shower." Vivien still wore her pajamas shorts. She suppressed a yawn and carried the lattes toward the office.

Lorna glanced up when Vivien entered. Her eyes rounded, and she instantly reached for a latte. Into the phone, she said, "Yes, Mrs. McDowell. There are one hundred and four seats so you can sell that many tickets for your event."

Sue held up the bag to show them. "I brought chocolate muffins too. Stu told me you all liked them."

"Oh, yes, Stu, you sweet, sweet crack dealer!" Vivien exclaimed.

Lorna made a small noise and threw a pencil at Vivien to get her attention.

"What?" Vivien asked, pretending to be offended as she rubbed her arm.

"I'm sure your church group will have a fantastic evening," Lorna said loudly into the phone, her eyes wide as she stared at Vivien.

"Oops," Vivien mumbled, slowly backing out of the office with the remaining lattes. She turned to go upstairs.

"No, I haven't seen that particular film. I'll have to hope you only sell one hundred and three tickets so I can sneak in the back to watch." Lorna pointed at the bag with a hopeful look on her face.

Sue pulled out a muffin and handed it to her.

Lorna grinned and mouthed, "Thank you."

Sue nodded and moved to follow Vivien to the apartment. Vivien had put the latte container on the kitchen island and lounged on a chair near the window.

Heather came from the bathroom in a flannel shirt and jeans. Her wet hair was wound into a bun at her neck.

"Stu sent muffin crack." Vivien reached for Sue's bag, wiggling her fingers. Sue handed it over.

"One day, you're going to call it that to the wrong person." Heather went for the coffee cup. "And I'm not going to say a word when they cart you off to jail."

"You're no fun," Vivien said. "That's okay. Sue will bail me out, won't you?"

"What took so long? Was there a long line today?" Heather asked, sitting by Vivien and taking her muffin from her to eat it herself.

"I know you didn't have trouble finding it." Vivien grinned, grabbing another muffin to replace the stolen one. "Was Jameson working this morning? Is that what happened?"

"There was a line, and I went to the bookstore." Sue took her latte and sat down at the table with them. "So I have some news."

Both women set their muffins down.

"I bought the bookstore today. Melba is going to stay on to show me how to run it." Sue took a deep breath and waited for their reactions. "Am I insane for doing this?"

"Ah..." Heather tilted her head to the side.

Vivien reached to take her hand. Slowly, she smiled. "Not at all. I feel very strongly that is exactly where you need to be."

"I think so too. It's funny. I walked in, and it became clear that I didn't want to leave this town." Sue took a nervous sip of her latte. "Ever since I put on the ring, it's like I've been hit with clarity. I came here. I met you all. I bought a bookstore."

"I didn't know Melba was finally selling," Heather said. "It's a great building. Quality crafts-manship. The wood floors could use some work, though. Say the word, and I'll have my brother help me refurbish them. It'll only take a weekend."

"Jameson owns the building, so we'd have to ask him. I'll only have the store," Sue admitted. "I hope that doesn't become awkward."

"Dating your landlord?" Vivien waved a hand in dismissal. "Go for it. You only live once."

Sue tried to hide her blush, but there was no hiding anything from Vivien.

"What?" Vivien demanded. "So help me if you buried the lead with that whole, I bought a bookstore story..."

"Vivien, for the record, you have a loud mouth." Lorna appeared at the top of the stairs with her latte and a half-eaten muffin. "By the way, you just scored yourself two tickets to Mrs. McDowell's slide show musical performance one-woman extravaganza."

"Yeah, I'm not going to that," Vivien dismissed.

"Well, she thinks you're a crack addict now," Lorna said. "She's praying for your soul."

"Shh, lecture me later," Vivien said. "Sue was about to dish."

"What's up? Was something happening at the coffee shop? You were gone a long time." Lorna asked, moving to sit on the couch. She leaned on the arm to face them.

"I bought the bookstore," Sue said. "I'm going to move to Freewild Cove."

Before Lorna could answer, Vivien said, "Not that. Tell us what happened with Jameson. Or do you want me to try to guess?"

Vivien started reaching for her.

Sue leaned back in her chair. "I had sex with Jameson. In his office. At the coffee shop. We locked the door. It was awesome."

Lorna's mouth dropped open. Heather laughed softly.

"You go you!" Vivien clapped her hand and

jumped up to do a little dance, singing a made up song, "Su-san. Getting freaky. With Jameson. In the coffee shop."

"Sit down." Heather tugged at Vivien's pajama shirt. "Too much action before full coffee levels are achieved."

"Does that make me a harlot or something?" Sue moaned and dropped her head on the table. "There were customers in the main area."

"Hell, no, that doesn't make you a harlot. That makes you my hero. Just because a woman likes sex doesn't mean she's any more whorish than her male counterparts," Vivien stated as she sat down. "Well done. Jameson's one hot catch."

"He's a sweetheart." Heather took a sip of her latte. "I was thinking about him in the shower—"

"Heather!" Vivien scolded in mock affront.

"Not like that. I was thinking about last night and I started remembering all the things I've heard about Jameson over the years. After what you were married to, you deserve a good man, Sue. Jameson is a good man. He's generous without bragging about it. Mary Turner told me he paid her overdue electric bill when her husband was out of work. It was supposed to be anonymous, but a lady in billing told her. I've heard several stories like that."

"Wait, so, you bought a bookstore and slept with Jameson?" Lorna shook her head. "And I thought I had a busy morning."

"I think it's cool you're moving to town," Heather said. "Welcome. This is clearly where you're meant to be. Julia's magic is never wrong. It's insane and sideways and annoying, but never wrong."

"Thank you." Sue glanced around. "I know you probably didn't plan on me being here forever. I want to talk to you about renting this apartment. I'm happy to sign a lease and make it official."

"No," Heather stated.

"Oh." Sue nodded. "I understand."

"I'm not renting it to you. You're going to live here as long as you want," Heather said.

"That doesn't feel right. I need to pay you something," Sue said.

"I tell you what." Heather picked a chocolate chip out of the muffin and tossed it into her mouth. "How about you tap into your amazing powers and help me clean whenever I have renters move out, or construction is over? It'll take you two minutes and save me thousands each year. That way we both win."

"Deal." Sue agreed.

"So, in his office," Vivien prompted, trying to get

the conversation back around to Jameson. "Was it on his desk?"

Sue covered her mouth and tried not to blush. She slowly nodded, laughing into her hand as she managed to say, "Yes."

"You naughty, naughty librarian," Vivien teased.

"It's always the quiet ones," Heather added.

"Um, I hate to be the downer," Lorna interrupted, "but what about the other problem?"

Sue's smile faded. "I told Jameson about Hank. He knows what happened. I didn't tell him that he's haunting me, though."

"That's probably wise," Vivien agreed. "Trust us. The whole magic and ghosts are real conversations aren't ones we've perfected yet. People tend to freak out, and you can't blame them."

"It's best people don't know. Most mean well, but they tell one person, then they tell one person, and soon it's not a secret, and we're back to being the local freak show," Heather said. "Viv and I spent our childhood under that microscope. I don't want to go back there."

Sue understood the desire to hide the truth. She'd hidden her reality from everyone for so long. There had been so much shame. She'd hidden it so well that no one ever believed her when she tried to talk about Hank. She didn't want to live like that anymore. Telling Jameson what happened, showing him who she was, had been life altering.

But Heather, Lorna, and Vivien's secrets were not hers to tell, and she could respect that.

Sue bit the inside of her lip and shook her head. "I'm so sorry, Heather. I don't know what got into me. It's like I couldn't stop myself long enough to think logically. I just acted on impulse and did what I wanted. First the bookstore, then I slept with Jameson, and then I told him magic was real. I didn't mention your names, though. Just me."

"Maybe he didn't believe you," Lorna said.

"I used it to pick up the office after we..." Sue gave a guilty sigh. "He was there. He knows about me. I'm sorry. I never meant to make your lives more difficult."

Heather slowly nodded and sat back in her seat. "What's done is done. We'll hope for the best. Thank you for not telling him directly about us."

"I won't. I promise," Sue said.

"I don't think we have to worry about Jameson," Vivien said. "It's like Martin and you. Martin knows about us because magic led him and his daughter to us, to you. Same with Troy and me. And well, William is a Warrick so of course he knows. Jameson is bound to learn about it sooner or later."

"I'm inclined to agree with Viv on this one," Lorna said. "We all know the power of the rings. If Sue felt like she needed to tell him, then she did. There is no use in fighting our destiny. It sounds like Jameson is a big part of hers."

"It's not the rings," Vivien corrected. "The magic is in us. The rings are talismans, a way to focus and amplify the energy inside us."

Thoughts of Hank began to cloud her, dampening the promise of the morning. She'd taken steps for a future, but that didn't mean her past wasn't still lingering, waiting to draw her back whether she wanted to go or not. She had not been able to fight him in life. How could she face him now, in death, when he had nothing to lose?

"I'm lucky to have met you all," Sue said. "I've never had friends like you."

Lorna went to her and hugged her around the shoulders. "We're happy to have met you too, Sue. Whatever comes, we're here for you. You're not alone."

Julia's words echoed in her mind. "*Some things others can't do for you. Remember that. Inner strength does not come from outside. It can't be given.*"

Sue struggled to keep the tears out of her eyes. She didn't want to cry. These women were so generous, so giving. She couldn't ask them to face Hank if he came back. Hank was her demon. Julia had told her she needed to confront him alone.

*"Others can't do for you."*

"Books and coffee." Vivien smiled, picking up her muffin as she changed the subject back to Sue and Jameson. "That's actually kind of poetic."

"I thought so," Sue agreed. "If I didn't freak him out, we have a date tonight."

Suddenly, she frowned.

"What?" Heather asked.

Sue glanced at her suitcase, still unpacked. "I don't have anything to wear on a date. When my television became possessed, and the remote started hovering in the air, I panicked. I threw some stuff into a suitcase, but it's like two outfits, twenty pairs of underwear, and that kitten shirt."

"That's why God invented stores," Vivien said. "And friends. You'll raid our closets. I'm sure we have plenty that will fit you until you can go shopping."

"That reminds me. It's laundry day for me," Lorna said. "We should go home. I need to be back here in a few hours to set up for the matinee."

## CHAPTER THIRTEEN

"Okay, I know I'm forty-whatever years old, but I still don't know what this extra crotch pocket is for." Heather held up a pair of panties she was folding. They sat in the living room of Old Anderson House doing laundry. Already they'd filled a basket of clothes Sue could borrow, a variety of outfits that looked nothing like her old life but a perfect combination to create something new.

Vivien glanced at Heather and answered with a straight face, "That's where I stash my vag cash for emergencies. Carrying a purse is so last century."

Sue covered her mouth as she choked on her surprised laugh.

"It's called a gusset," Lorna answered, folding a towel. "It's to make underwear more comfortable on the lady parts by covering seams or lace. Also, it's breathable, so you don't get yeast infections."

"I kind of hate that you know the real answer," Vivien made a face at Lorna. She'd spent more time going through the piles looking for clothes for Sue than actually folding them. "I think vagina cash is—"

"That's horrifying. I'm going to start knocking." A man held up his hands and slowly backed out of the living room doorway. Windblown brown hair framed a handsome face. His looks made it obvious he and Heather were related.

"William, wait..." Lorna pushed up from the couch and moved to the window. She frowned as she saw his truck leaving the driveway. "He left without me."

"He'll drive around the block and be back." Heather continued folding her clothes. "He thinks he's funny."

"We should talk about tampons when he comes back," Vivien suggested. Suddenly, she stood. "That reminds me, Lorna. I bought you a gift."

"Tampons reminded you to give me something?" Lorna arched a brow and joked, "Now I'm horrified."

Vivien opened a couple of boxes before finding what she was looking for. She tossed a small plastic bag at Lorna. "Housewarming gift. You're welcome."

Lorna looked at the bag's logo. "From a truck stop?"

Vivien nodded. "Open it."

Lorna pulled out a condom-sized packet and read, "*French tickler.*"

"They were selling them from vending machines in the bathroom," Vivien answered. "It made me think of you."

"Gee. You shouldn't have," Heather drawled.

"Don't be jealous. I got you love gel." Vivien produced another bag and tossed it at Heather. "It's banana flavored."

"Eww." Heather grimaced.

"Sorry, Sue, we hadn't met when I got these, but next time." Vivien sat back down.

"That's okay," Sue said.

"Now everyone can have a date night tonight with their manfriends." Vivien reached to Lorna's pile and took a couple of folded towels. She handed them to Sue. "You'll need these, too."

"What do you think it's like to be a ghost," Lorna asked. "I mean, Julia is lucid and seems to feel things. Do you think they feel like we feel, or is it just a residual motivational energy type thing? I'm not sure I'd like being like that forever."

"I would," Vivien said. "I want to experience

everything, even the afterlife. Though, I'd have to be lucid like Julia, not some moaning phantom doing the same thing over and over, trapped in a loop."

"What would you do as a lucid ghost?" Sue asked. "Help people?"

Vivien laughed. "I like to think that ghost me would take the high road and try to help the living like solving crimes or whatnot, but if I'm honest, I know I'll mess with people all the time. And maybe haunt the men's showers at the gym or something fun like that."

"That's the second time someone mentioned ghosts and showers. Julia said the same thing. I might never bathe again," Sue said.

"Try not to think about it," Lorna advised.

The door opened, and William came back inside. "Is it over?"

Lorna smiled, instantly standing to greet him. "Fair warning, Vivien's on a roll but don't leave. I need that ride to work. Let me grab my purse, and then we can go."

Lorna ran upstairs.

"Hi Willy." Vivien smiled at him and wiggled her fingers. "How are you?"

"Has Vivien been day drinking again?" William

asked Heather. He remained standing as he waited for Lorna to return.

"I've only had one glass of red wine last night before bed," Vivien said. "That's the perfect amount to get all the benefits with none of the badifits."

"Badifits?" William arched a brow. "Please tell me you know that's not a real thing."

Sue knew William was Heather's brother, but he and Vivien bickered like siblings.

"Do you want to see the present I got Lorna?" Vivien offered.

"No." William shook his head in denial. "Definitely not."

"Hey, you didn't get a chance to meet Sue, yet, have you?" Heather interrupted. "Sue, this is my brother William. Will, Sue is one of us. She just bought the bookstore downtown."

His eyes went to the ring on her hand, and he took a deep breath as if seeing it confirmed something for him. "Hi Sue."

"Nice to meet you," Sue answered.

"And she's dating Jameson Lloyd," Vivien interjected.

"Really?" William nodded. "Jameson's a good guy. He helped me change a tire on my truck a few months back. I picked up a nail at one of the construction sites."

"That reminds me." Heather reached to take a notepad and pen out of her flannel shirt pocket and spoke as she scribbled, "Buy nails."

"I got a bunch in the truck," William said. "What kind you need?"

"Masonry," Heather said.

"Sure, they're in the toolbox." William motioned that his sister should follow him. "Take as many as you need."

"Awesome, that saves me a trip." Heather joined him, and they went outside.

"What's this I hear from Butch about one of your genius tenants tapping into a sewer pipe to fill a hot tub?" William asked.

"It wasn't the sewer," Heather said before her voice became too far away to hear.

"He seems nice," Sue said.

"I've known William practically our whole lives." Vivien studied Sue. "Heather meant it when she said you're one of us."

Sue didn't answer.

"I felt a twinge like you still think you're interrupting our lives or an intruder." Vivien shook her head. "You're not, you know. There is plenty of room in our lives for one more friend."

Sue nodded. "Thank you."

A phone dinged. Vivien sighed and sat back in her chair. She produced her cell phone from beside her hip and began scrolling.

Lorna came downstairs. She looked around the front room and frowned. "Viv, did you chase my ride off again?"

Vivien waved her hand in dismissal. "He's outside getting nails for Heather." She started typing on her phone.

Lorna took a deep breath and fanned her face. She moved to look at the thermostat on the wall. "Is anyone else hot? I would have sworn it was ninety degrees in here."

"I think it's okay," Sue answered when Vivien kept reading her phone, frowning.

"Viv?" Lorna asked.

Vivien turned off her screen and looked up. "Fry cook was horsing around last night. He slipped and hit his head. They took him to the emergency room. He's fine. A couple of stitches. I sent a group text to all of the managers for a mandatory safety meeting again."

"I'm glad to hear he's not seriously hurt," Lorna

said. "Let me know if that changes. We can take a trip wherever he is and help."

"I think he's wearing the stitches as a badge of honor," Vivien said. "The manager told me the others gave him the nickname Slippy. He's been asking for the security tapes so he can put the video on social media."

"Ah, teenagers," Lorna chuckled. "Gotta love 'em."

"What were you asking?" Vivien turned her full attention to Lorna.

"Oh, I was just saying I thought it was hot in here." Lorna lifted her arms and fanned her armpits for effect. "I'm on my period and sweating under my boobs."

"I really need to start knocking before I walk in here," William said from the doorway with a rueful shake of his head. "Ready, my love?"

"Coming." Lorna moved to follow him. Before she left, she said to Vivien, "Hot flashes suck ass. Fuck growing old empowerment. We were wrong." As she walked through the door, she cried playfully, "Retreat, retreat, retreat!"

"You're wrong. We're awesome, beautiful, strong creatures," Vivien yelled after her. "Don't you forget it."

"Look who I found," Heather said, coming back inside.

Sue had met January briefly when Martin stopped by the theater to drop her off. The ten-year-old girl looked a lot like her father. It wasn't just her dark hair and eyes, but the way she carried herself. She wore a long-sleeve t-shirt and cargo pants that had tiny splatters of white paint on them like she'd been working on a construction site. She carried a backpack.

"Hey there, Jan," Vivien said. "Are you hanging out with us today?"

The girl nodded. "Heather, can I read in the tower?"

"Sure," Heather said. "Say hi to Sue first."

"Hey, Sue." Jan frowned.

"Hi January," Sue answered, smiling. "What's the tower?"

Jan shrugged and edged away from her.

"Cupola," Vivien answered. "That small thing on the top of the house. It served as a lookout toward the ocean."

Jan tugged at Heather's hand and whispered none too softly, "Whose that angry guy with her? He looks mean."

Sue shot up from her chair and spun around. Her

heart leaped in her chest, and she found it hard to breathe. She didn't see or smell anything.

"It's nothing. We're taking care of it. Head on up," Heather urged the girl.

"Can I help with the exorcism?" Jan asked.

"Not with this one," Heather said. "Maybe next time. Go on."

January ran up the stairs two at a time.

Vivien had also stood. "Heather?"

"I don't see anything." Heather frowned.

"I should go," Sue said. "It's not safe for me to be here."

"Nonsense," Vivien denied.

Sue glanced toward the ceiling. "Not with Jan here."

Vivien nodded. "Grab the clothes. We'll go to the theater."

"I'll call Martin and have him come back to pick her up," Heather said.

"Nonsense," Vivien denied. "You can't see him, and if we're not allowed to séance him, there is nothing we can do but wait. That girl needs your steady presence. Besides, if Hank is popping in unannounced and unnoticed, we need you to start applying any protection measures you can think of to keep danger out of this place. Smudge the whole damn house until smoke is rolling out of the windows, and it looks like it's on fire if you have to."

"Call me if you need me," Heather said.

"We will." Vivien helped Sue carry the clothes to the car. "I know you're worried, but I promise, we'll figure this out."

They kept saying that, but Sue wasn't so sure they would figure it out. None of them had realized Hank had been in the room with them. Was he beside her even now? She glanced back at the house to see January watching her from a third-story window. Sue tried to smile at the girl in reassurance. Seeing ghosts at that age couldn't be easy. The child's worried expression didn't change.

"Let's go," Vivien said, slamming her trunk shut.

Sue jumped at the sound and hurried to get in the car.

## CHAPTER FOURTEEN

"I don't want to hear any excuses. That is fear talking. You're going on this date tonight." Vivien held up two dress choices—a red and a black. "You can't live your life in fear of what Hank's ghost is going to do."

Sue shook her head, not moving from her place on the bed. Her wet hair hung around her face. She'd taken a shower, which was a nerve-racking feat considering she kept imagining perverted spirits watching her. Now she sat wrapped in a towel, watching Vivien pick out an outfit for her date.

"Hank is an abuser. He's selfish, narcissistic, and only cares about himself. That is what those types are like. In his mind, if he can't have you, no one can." Vivien dropped the red dress and tried to hand Sue the black one. "He wants you scared and hiding. He doesn't want you out there having fun and living your life. This is your chance to kick him in the cosmic balls and tell him to go fuck himself all the way to hell."

"Jan said he was angry. I know what he's like when he's angry. There is no reasoning with him. What if he tries to hurt Jameson?" Sue hadn't thought things through when she'd slept with Jameson. What if Hank saw? What if he knew? "What if he hurts you, or Lorna, or Heather? I can't live with that. I have been thinking, and maybe it's best I go back to St. Louis by myself."

Vivien dropped the hand holding the dress. The slinky black material bunched on the bed. "Try it."

"What?" Sue asked in surprise at her tone.

"I said try it." Vivien pursed her lips together and arched a brow.

Sue lowered her gaze.

"You are our friend, Sue. You might not believe that yet or understand that true friends are always there for each other no matter what, but we're not going anywhere. You can go back to St. Louis, but you're delusional if you think I won't jump into the car and follow you there." She again held up the dress. "I think you should wear this one."

A tear slipped down her cheek. "No one has ever fought for me before."

"Tell me this. If a demon was going after Lorna, or a spirit convinced Jan to burn down Heather's house, or my first husband kept trying to lure me to my death in the ocean, would you just step back and let it happen? Or would you do all you could to help?"

"That's a silly question," Sue said. "Of course, I'd help."

"There you go." Vivien took the black dress off the hanger and tossed it at Sue. "So you do get it. We're friends. That's what friends do."

Sue sighed and pulled the dress off her head. She couldn't argue with Vivien's logic. Vivien turned her back so Sue could get dressed.

Sue stood by the bed and dropped the towel. "Julia mentioned a demon crossing over with Lorna's husband. Is that what happened?"

"It was our first séance. We made a mistake. Don't worry, we vanquished it," Vivien answered.

Sue slipped the dress over her head. "And the fire?"

"Heather's son wanted her to move on. He was ten when he died. Let's just say he and Jan, in all their ten-year-old wisdom, decided if they burned down the house, then Heather would have to literally move on."

"That's so sad," Sue said. "I feel that pain in her when we touch."

"Things like that can never completely heal," Vivien said. "It's a part of her now. She's doing better, though, now that she had a chance to say goodbye to him."

"And you? Your first husband tried to drown you in the ocean?"

Vivien glanced over her shoulder. Seeing Sue had the dress on, she twirled her finger to indicate Sue should turn around. When she did, Vivien reached for the zipper.

"Not on purpose. Sam was trying to lead me to a bottle that he had buried in the sand. The most direct route was through the water to the beach across the way from my old house." Vivien zipped the dress and turned Sue by her shoulders. She gave an approving nod. "I knew that dress would look great on you, better than it looks on me. You should keep it."

Sue moved toward the bathroom to look in a mirror. The gown hugged her body with the skirt flaring around her hips to create a nice flow when she walked. The neckline plunged between her breasts, teasing without revealing too much.

"It's beautiful, thank you," Sue said.

"You make the dress." Vivien went back to the clothing bags she'd brought in. "I have some shoes for you to try in here somewhere."

Sue's phone started to vibrate on the counter. Vivien went to check it for her. "Kathy."

"Hank's mother. Don't answer," Sue said.

Vivien silenced the call. She began snooping through Sue's phone. "This woman has called you thirty-six times, left twenty-three voice mails, and," Vivien pushed at the screen, "she's been rage messaging."

"I know. I'll call her later."

"You don't have to," Vivien said. She held up the phone to show the text message screen was open. "Do you mind?"

Sue shook her head in denial. She didn't care if Vivien read them. At this point, the woman knew all her secrets.

"*Call me, call me, call me,*" Vivien read quickly in a bored voice. "*You're being selfish. Pick up the phone. Have you found the cufflinks? How can you treat me like this? Hank would be appalled. How can you embarrass me like this? Don't you dare sell Hank's cufflinks. I want them. He's my boy. You're useless. You didn't deserve my saint of a son.*"

"She's a piece of work," Sue said, not wanting to hear more.

Vivien lowered the phone. "Can I call her?"

Sue laughed. "Why would you want to do that?"

"I'm calling her." Vivien hit the callback button and held the phone to her ear.

Sue rushed to her side and leaned in to listen. Vivien put it on speakerphone as it rang.

"Where the hell have you been, Susan?" Kathy didn't bother to say hello as she launched into an angry tirade. "Do you know how humiliated I was when you didn't come to Hank's dinner honoring him for his great service to this community?"

"I hear a lot of me and I statements in there, Kathy," Vivien said.

"What?" Kathy asked in confusion. "Who is this?"

"You can call me Mrs. Stone," Vivien stated. "I'm a friend of Sue's. I want you to listen to me very, very carefully, Kathy."

"Wha—?" Kathy tried to protest.

"Shh," Vivien cut her off. "Now, Kathy, I think we both know that your son was not the perfect angel you claim he was. You raised a murderous, wife-beating asshole who got what he deserved when he hit Sue with a hammer and tried to dump her body."

Kathy gasped.

"I am sensitive to the fact that he's your son, and you love him, but Sue doesn't. She spent years taking his abuse while you turned a blind eye. She doesn't want to talk about him. If the fact she has not picked up the phone when you call hasn't clued you in, let me enlighten you. She doesn't want to hear from you at all. I'm going to need you to stop calling and texting this number. Don't go over to the house. Don't expect Sue at any dinner parties. She will not be over for the holidays. If I so much as hear you breathe Sue's name, I will hire a ghostwriter, and we'll publish a tell-all about every dirty little thing your son did, and I won't change names to protect anyone. I'll hand a copy to every last person in St. Louis. Do we have an understanding, Kathy? Leave Sue alone, and I'll leave this story alone. I'm sorry for your loss."

Sue stared at Vivien in wonder. Her mouth fell open.

"Oh, and I flushed the cufflinks down the toilet. Sorry." Vivien hung up the phone and set it on the counter.

Sue stared in amazement. "I can't believe you said that to her."

"I doubt you'll hear from her again," Vivien went back to looking for the shoes.

"She can have the cuff links. I don't want them. I don't want anything that belonged to him."

"She doesn't deserve the cuff links. I say sell everything and use the seed money to get the life you deserve. Turn it into something positive," Vivien said. "When I heard her speaking to you like that, I suddenly just knew her greatest fear. She didn't want anything tarnishing that perfect image she's tried so hard to cultivate. Even if she doesn't admit the truth to herself, a part of her knows who her son was. She won't want that information out there."

Sue felt like a giant weight lifted off her chest. "I thought I'd have to change my name and number to get her to stop."

Vivien produced a pair of red heels. "Put these on."

Sue pulled the shoes on and rocked them back and forth. "They're a little snug."

"Slip your feet out of them and stretch your toes when you're sitting at the table," Vivien said. "Trust me. You look hot in them. He won't be able to resist you."

Sue laughed. "They're a little high. I'm not used to heels like these."

"Practice walking in them," Vivien said, draping the discarded dresses over her arm. "Show Lorna the dress. Her matinee crowd should be gone by now. I'll put some of these clothes away so they don't wrinkle, and then we'll do your hair and makeup."

Sue carefully walked across the apartment and down the steps. The lights were dim in the lobby, and the theater was quiet. When they arrived, people had been inside watching an old black and white movie.

Lorna wasn't in her office. On impulse, Sue concentrated on the office and motioned her finger. She watched as it cleaned itself. If the bookstore didn't work out, she'd start a maid service.

Lifting her head, she practiced strolling across the lobby. The sun had already set outside, but street-lights made it easy to see beyond the glass. She stopped, nervously looking at the door where Hank had appeared. Instead, she saw her reflection standing in the black dress and red heels. She hardly recognized herself.

Hearing a loud thud coming from the theater, Sue went to find Lorna. She pushed through the curtains, peeking to make sure the movie was over. The screen was dark, and the seats were empty. She heard another thud.

"Hey, Lorna? Are you in here? I need your

honest opinion about this dress." Sue walked down the aisle toward the stage.

Her hand began to tingle. She slowed her steps and looked around.

"Lorna?"

No one answered.

"Julia?" Sue whispered. "Is that you?"

She took a few more steps.

"Sue?" Jameson's voice came from behind. He sounded breathless as he hurried toward her. He gripped his phone in his hand. "I ran here as fast as I could. What's the matter? What's wrong?"

"What do you mean?" Sue again glanced around the seating area.

"Your text." He slowed his steps.

A creak sounded overhead. They both glanced up, but she didn't see anything.

"Jameson, I didn't text you," she said

"You texted 'danger help'," he insisted.

"No, I—"

A dark laugh sounded, projected from the stage. Fear shot through her. Sue turned quickly and stumbled on her high heels. She caught herself before she fell.

A loud *pop-pop* sounded. Sue looked at the

ceiling in time to see a blur of movement coming toward her.

"Watch out!" Jameson yelled.

He slammed against her, pulling her out of the way. The theater lights crashed where she'd been standing. The sound of striking metal and breaking glass reverberated in the auditorium. His arm hooked her waist, and he kept running with her toward the stage. Her heels fell off as she stumbled, leaving her barefoot.

Jameson stopped but didn't let go. "Are you all right?"

Sue nodded. Her heart hammered violently. She stared at the large, broken fixture with its sharp protruding edges.

"Did it get you?" he insisted, grabbing her face to check her for injuries.

"You saved my life." Sue threw her arms around his neck. She shook violently. The ring on her hand vibrated with a warning. A loud, frantic thud sounded from far away as if someone banged on the walls.

Remembering the laugh, she pushed away from him to look at the stage. The smell of gun oil and cedar assaulted them.

Jameson coughed. "Where is that coming from?"

"You can't be here." Sue tried to push him across a row of seats to the other aisle, to where the path was a little clearer. "It's not safe."

"What are you talking about?" He refused to budge. "Sue, what's going on here."

Sue looked around, trying to catch any hint of where Hank might be so she could send Jameson in the opposite direction.

"You won't believe me," Sue answered. "You need to get out of here."

"Come with me. I'm not leaving you," Jameson denied, refusing to go when she pushed harder at him.

"He's angry at me." Sue coughed as the smell of the cologne became so thick her eyes watered. The taste of it choked her, and she recognized the bourbon.

"What is that?" Jameson looked around, gagging as he covered his mouth.

"Smell, taste," Sue whispered in mounting panic. "Jameson, please, go."

"Who's after you?"

"I can't..." Sue realized he wasn't going to go on his own, so she grabbed his hand and pulled him into the seats toward the other aisle.

Suddenly, the seat bottoms at the end of the row began slamming up and down hard, moving like a wave toward them. She pushed back into him but didn't make it out in time. A cushioned seat bottom sprang forward. The hard plastic frame knocked her into the seat in front of it. She cried out as pain radiated from her thigh and stomach. It felt as bad as when Hank had punched her.

Jameson pulled her out of the row and into his arms. Over the loud banging seats, he yelled, "I'll believe you!"

"It's Hank," she yelled.

His expression instantly turned from confusion to anger.

"He's haunting me," Sue cried. "You have to get out of here. It's me he wants!"

"I'm not leaving you. We're getting out of here together." Jameson refused to let her go. He pulled her with him toward the stage stairs.

When they reached the stage, the chairs stopped banging. The silence was just as terrifying. Sue held on to Jameson's hand, and they took a slow step across the stage. They both searched around the area, glancing up at the ceiling for any weapons Hank might use against them.

"Sue?" Heather ran into the auditorium only to

stop when she saw the lighting rig blocking her path. "Hold on. We're coming around!"

Heather ran back out.

When they made it to center stage, the hum of the projector sounded, and a bright, flickering light came at them from the projection booth. Sue automatically turned to the movie screen. Their shadows cast as a black ring blipped around them to mark the start of a film.

A woman's giant face appeared in black-and-white, as she gasped, *"You think—"*

The screen instantly blipped again to a 1970s schoolchild who yelled, *"—I don't know—"*

It flicked to a cowboy, *"—what—"*

Then a silent film where the sheik mouthed the word, *"—head—"*

Then a construction worker, *"—move ahead—"*

The screen images began flickering too fast to register all the genres of films and faces, but the sound came in a rush of different, clipped voices, *"—head—head—head—head—what's in—your head—know—know—head—"*

"Stop it!" Sue screamed, covering her ears.

"Sue, we're coming!" Heather ran toward her. Vivien helped Lorna behind her as if the woman had trouble staying upright as she held her forehead.

Seats ripped from the ground and went flying at the wall where Vivien, Heather, and Lorna tried to approach. The women ducked back to safety.

"Get out of here," Sue screamed. "Save yourselves!"

Suddenly the scene from a low budget porno appeared. A woman leaned over a desk as her boss spanked her with his wooden desk nameplate. Each strike elicited a loud, sexual noise.

Sue gripped Jameson's hand tighter. Her eyes moved down to their shadows; only now there were three of them standing on the stage.

Sue turned toward the third shadow, but no one was there.

"Sue?" Jameson started to pull her hand.

She looked back at the screen in time to see the shadow's arm swinging at them. Jameson's hand ripped from her grasp as he flew across the stage. He hit the wall with a loud, ugly thud.

She glanced to where the shadow indicated Hank stood and then to the screen. She held up her hands as if to stop his advances.

"Do you see him?" Vivien's voice asked. They hadn't listened to her when she told them to leave.

"No," Heather answered.

"Sue, be careful!" Vivien yelled.

Sue kept her attention on the shadow's movement as it loomed toward her. It grew taller as if to tower over her.

"Hank, you don't have to do this." Sue desperately tried to reason, even though she knew it had never worked in the past. That same old fear filled her. Her side ached from where she'd slammed into the chair. Tears rolled down her face. "Please, just let me go. It's over. Let me go."

The shadow swung. She tried to dodge, but a formidable force smacked her across the face. She cried out as she fell to the floor. Hank usually tried to avoid her face so no one saw the bruises, but now that he was dead, maybe he'd stopped caring. The shadow moved over her. She tried to block a kick, but the invisible blow tossed her onto her back.

Sue coughed, and the taste of blood entered her mouth.

Hank kicked her again. She tried to stop him, but there was no blocking a ghost. She knew each blow would bring her closer to death. Hank had come for her like she knew he would, and he would not stop until she was dead.

The clipped series of voices returned, "*I know—what's in—your head—know—know—whore—know—if I can't have you—no one can—no— your head—*"

And then the porno resumed playing. The woman gasped in loud pleasure as she was hit over and over, the scene repeating itself on a loop.

Sue saw her friends edging their way onto the stage behind Hank's shadow. She caught a glimpse of Lorna's bloody face.

It was one thing to beat her. It was another to hurt her friends and her new beau.

Years of anger and fear exploded inside of Sue. She screamed, charging up from the floor with a strength she didn't know she had.

"You will not hurt them," she cried. "You will not hurt them, you fucking asshole!"

She swung blindly toward where the shadow appeared to be, punching her arms like a madwoman. She felt her fists hitting a cold mass and kept pounding.

"I hate you," Sue yelled.

Hank's presence seemed to fall to the floor. She saw his shadow on his back on the screen next to them. She kept hitting toward the cold spot. Her legs straddled Hank's ghost, keeping him penned where she could strike him. Her hand stung and bled like she punched ice, but she didn't care.

"I hate you. I hate you. I hate your smell. I hate your taste. I hate your laugh. I hate that stupid joke you make about Hank Jewel's family jewels. No one thinks that's funny." Sue didn't think, as the anger and hurt rolled out of her in a storm of pent up rage. "I hate your smile. I hate the way you make me feel. I hate you. I hate you. I hate you, you infantile, stupid, prick!"

"Sue," Jameson's weak voice croaked from behind her.

Her punches became weaker, and she panted for breath, but she didn't stop trying to hurt Hank.

"You don't hurt the people I care about," she gasped.

Heather rushed to Sue's side and grabbed her right arm. Sue tried to pull free to keep hitting Hank, but Heather held tight. Sue struck him with her left fist.

Vivien supported Lorna as they joined them. Lorna's eyes appeared dazed, but she reached for Heather's hand. Vivien kept hold of Lorna and grabbed Sue's left arm. The ring on her finger sent a pulse of energy through her, and their presence gave her strength.

In unison, the three women yelled over the porno, "Beings tethered to this plane, full of rage and filled with pain. We call you to come near. We call you to face what you fear. We call you to your eternal hell. Pay the price with this final knell."

Tiny lights erupted beneath Sue, filling in the details of Hank's transparent face. His eyes were wide, and he looked terrified. It spread quickly through his body, revealing him. Vivien let go of her, and Heather tried to pull Sue to her feet. Jameson appeared next to them, taking over for Heather as he lifted Sue from on top of Hank. He held her against his chest, an arm hooked under her knees and the other behind her back.

Rage distorted Hank's face as he yelled, writhing on the floor. The movie image appeared to melt like film under fire, leaving a white screen. The light inside him grew, turning an angry, burning red.

"Spirit," Vivien muttered in disgust, "we release you."

Hank's mouth opened as if he would yell, but instead, his body exploded into a surge of flames that quickly turned into dying embers. The lights drifted to the stage floor and went out.

The smell of Hank's cologne instantly disappeared, and Sue took a deep breath. She felt the fear and anger inside her die with him.

Jameson held her tight as he stared at the floor.

Sue reached for his face and forced him to turn to her. "Are you hurt?"

He shook his head in denial, but she suspected he might be lying. Hank had thrown him against the wall pretty hard.

Sue squirmed to be let down. Jameson acted as if he didn't want to let her go but finally set her on her feet. She cradled her ribs with her sore arm. Both hands throbbed where she had punched the skin raw.

"Lorna?" Sue stumbled to where Lorna sat on the floor, holding her head in her hands. Jameson followed close behind, not leaving her side.

"Bastard pushed the storage shelf on me," she grumbled.

"I'm so sorry," Sue whispered. "The last thing I wanted was for any of you to get hurt."

Lorna looked up at her. "You didn't do this. I'll be fine."

"Heather? Vivien?" Sue asked.

"I'm good," Vivien said.

"I'm so glad I ignored you guys and came," Heather said. "I just had this feeling like I needed to be here."

Lorna took in Sue's face. She looked to where Sue cradled her arms across her stomach. When she opened her mouth to say something about it, the sound of clapping came from the destroyed auditorium.

Jameson automatically put himself in front of Lorna and Sue and held his arms out to create a human shield.

Heather walked to the edge of the stage and stared into the wreckage. "Julia says to tell you great performance. The best show she's seen in a long time."

Sue leaned to look around Jameson's legs, but she couldn't see Julia.

"She said she's glad you got her text?" Heather glanced back, not understanding.

"Who are you talking to?" Jameson asked.

Heather scrunched up her face and turned back to the seats. "I will *not* ask him to do that!"

"What?" Jameson turned to look at Sue.

"It's fine. She's talking to her grandma." Sue reached her wrist to him so he could help pull her up without touching her injured hands.

"Is Hank gone?" Heather asked the auditorium. "Grandma, is Hank's ghost—*fine!*"

Heather turned to Jameson.

"What?" he asked.

"Could you..." She frowned, sighing. "I'm so sorry. Could you like twirl around so my dead grandma can get a look at you? It's the only way she'll answer me if Hank is gone for good."

"Uh..." Jameson looked at Sue, who gave him an apologetic smile. He lifted his arms to the side and slowly turned around. When his butt was toward the chairs, the clapping sounded anew. He quickly finished his turn and stepped closer to Sue. She leaned into him.

"Is Hank gone?" Heather asked before letting loose a long breath. "Yes. He's gone. You did it, Sue. You beat him."

Sue glanced at her bloody hands and muttered, "Pun intended?"

Heather gave a wry smile and turned back to her grandma. "I will not ask him to take off his shirt."

"Am I being," Jameson hesitated, "ogled by a ghost?"

"Get used to it," Vivien chuckled. "If you're going to be hanging around Sue, we're all part of the package."

"No, we will not start screening more of those sexy movies," Heather denied in exasperation.

Sue touched his face gently with her sore hand. "I'll understand if this is too much for you. I know we haven't known each other very long, and this is a lot of baggage."

Jameson glanced to where Hank had gone up in flames. "From what I see, you just set fire to most of it. I think maybe I'd like to help you carry the rest."

"That's either very sweet or very corny," Vivien said, patting Jameson on the shoulder.

"Sweet," Sue answered.

"A little corny," Jameson admitted.

"Thank you for saving my life," Sue said.

"Thank you for saving mine," he answered.

"Julia says it's over. Sue, you faced your inner demon and beat the living hell out of it. She wants me to tell you how proud she is of you and how you're worthy of wearing the ring. She also approves of you being with Jameson. I'm paraphrasing. Her version included references to nudity." Heather glanced around. "Anyone have questions before she goes?"

"Actually, I do have a question," Sue stated, moving to stand by Heather at the edge of the stage. Every inch of her ached. "What the hell is a Chicago overcoat?"

Lorna and Vivien laughed.

"I have absolutely no idea," Heather answered, shaking her head. "Julia has disappeared."

"Look at this place," Vivien said. "It's trashed."

"I got this." Sue lifted an injured hand and willed

the theater to write itself. She felt the ring pulse to amplify her magic.

The floors creaked and moaned. Suddenly, chairs began flying back into place. Bolts followed them, screwing themselves into the floor. She gestured again, and the lights lifted to the ceiling. She felt the energy draining out of her as each magical act took from her strength, but it was too late to stop it.

Sue swayed on her feet, falling to the side. Jameson caught her, and the world went black.

## CHAPTER FIFTEEN

SUE OPENED her eyes to see Jameson's face leaning over her. She was on the bed in the apartment. Warmth flooded her side, and she glanced over to see Lorna sitting beside them. Before she could register what was happening, the pain in her cheek lessened and Jameson's face bruised in her place.

"No." Sue pulled her arm away from Lorna.

"Too late," Lorna answered, standing gingerly as she held her stomach.

Vivien and Heather stood at the foot of the bed, each with one bruised hand. Sue lifted her hands to find them sore but partially healed.

When Sue would protest them taking her pain as their own, Vivien said, "It's what friends do. You'd do the same for us."

A tear slipped over Sue's tired cheek. She nodded. "So everything is good?"

"Your magic repaired the theater better than it was before," Heather said. "All the spotlights work now so that's something."

Sue smiled and nodded. "I'm glad."

"I left you some candy. Eat it. You'll feel better." Vivien stiffly turned. "I'm going home where Troy can take care of me."

Heather smiled at Sue and said, "You're free. There is nothing more to fear."

"Thank you," Sue mouthed, touched by their selfless generosity.

Heather limped as she followed Vivien. "Wait up, Viv."

"They're my ride," Lorna stated. "Are you going to be all right if we leave?"

"I'll stay with her," Jameson said before Sue could answer. "I won't leave her side."

"Call me if either of you needs me," Lorna ordered.

Sue and Jameson both nodded. Lorna ambled after Vivien and Heather, who could be heard slowly stepping down the stairs.

Jameson crawled over her and fell next to her on the bed. The mattress bounced, and they both groaned. He shifted his body and pulled a box of theater candy out from under him.

"Eat this," he said, not lifting his head as he pushed it toward her.

"Maybe later." Sue slipped her hand on top of his to hold it.

They laid in silence for a long time. Suddenly, Jameson gave a pained laugh.

"What?" Sue turned her head toward him.

He laid on his back, looking over at her. "This is the strangest first date I've ever been on. The bar had been set pretty high. I was just wondering how was going to top it on our next date."

"Apocalypse?" Sue suggested.

"Zombie horde?" he countered.

"Take down an international spy syndicate?"

"Alien invasion?"

"Striptease for grandma ghost?"

He smirked and shook his head in denial. "How about free coffee and a discount on the bookstore lease in exchange for your help cleaning the coffee shop?"

"Lease agreements are hot. So hot," Sue joked. She chuckled and instantly regretted it as the motion jarred her ribs. "It's a date."

Jameson slid his hand out from under hers and placed it on top. He lifted his head and moaned.

"What?" she asked.

"The light switch is really far away," he answered.

Sue closed her eyes, letting the exhaustion take her. "Leave it."

"Okay," he mumbled. His hand lightly patted hers. "Know in my mind I'm kissing you goodnight."

"And I'm kissing you back." Sue felt happiness flooding her. This was the life she wanted. Even with the pain, she wouldn't trade this moment for anything.

# CHAPTER SIXTEEN
## EPILOGUE

*St. Louis, Missouri*

Sue stood on the lawn and stared at the home she had shared with Hank. She couldn't help the sick feeling that filled her when she tried to go inside. In many ways, it was like excavating a puss-filled wound. Doing it sucked, but afterward, it felt great.

"Eww," Vivien appeared next to her. "I just had the weirdest visual, like I was about to pop a giant zit."

Sue suppressed a laugh. "Yeah, that is weird."

A car pulled up in front of the house.

"This must be the realtor. Let me get a read off her before you say yes to the contract. I'll walk with her around the property to give you a moment to collect yourself inside and do a quick..." Vivien made a whirling noise and swirled her hands around to indicate Sue's cleaning abilities.

Sue nodded. "Make sure she knows I'm motivated to sell. I want this book closed and tossed in the trash heap. I also don't want to come back for the closing."

"Gotcha." Vivien went to greet the woman.

"You don't have to go in if you don't want." Jameson came from the car carrying the purse she'd forgotten in the back seat. "Tell me what you want me to get. I'll take care of it."

Vivien and Jameson had insisted on coming with her, and she had never been more appreciative to have company. They'd made a road trip out of it, and their support had made the idea of coming back here bearable. Heather and Lorna had wanted to make the trip as well, but someone had to watch the theater, and Martin needed Heather's help with January.

"I'll be all right." Sue slipped her arm around his waist. "Thank you for coming with me."

"There is no way I'd let you face this alone." Jameson held her hand as they went to the front door.

Sue dug in her purse for her house keys to unlock the home. Inside, the air was stale, like time had stopped and waited for her to return. She had thought about what items she would want to keep. There weren't many.

The home was as she left it, the living room messed up from the supernatural scare. Sue waved her hand, forcing the room to clean itself. The cord hanging from the television plugged itself into the wall. She couldn't help watching it to see if it would try to send her messages. It remained off.

"Do you want me to start building moving boxes?" he asked. They were currently lying flat in his trunk. He'd insisted on bringing some just in case she needed them.

Sue didn't answer him as she went to the kitchen. Dust had settled on the surfaces. She was a little surprised that Kathy had not been coming to the house to clean. When Hank was alive, she'd been a constant source of housekeeping criticisms. She also hadn't called again. Apparently, Vivien's threats had worked and Sue was now free of the woman.

Sue lifted her hand, magically cleaning the kitchen. The dishwasher opened, and a load of dishes she'd left inside flew to their respective cabinets and drawers. Dust swirled and went into the trashcan. Items inside the drawers rattled as they straightened.

When everything settled, she went to a cabinet and pulled out a vase. She handed it to Jameson to carry. "This was my mother's. I don't want anything else in here."

Sue then pulled out trash bags and set them on the counter. She threw away a half-drunken bottle of wine that had been sitting out.

Jameson set the vase down and helped her clear out the fridge. When it was empty, she waved her hand and cleaned it as well. She made her way through the house quickly, cleaning each room, throwing away what needed to go, and leaving everything else behind. The last room was the bedroom.

"Can you get the duffle bag for my clothes, please?"

Jameson instantly went to do as she asked.

Sue stood alone in the bedroom and waved her hand to clean it. The bed made itself, and dust flew into the trash bag she held open.

Hank's smiling face stared at her from a photograph of them together. Sue didn't even feel the need to tell him to fuck off anymore. This part of her life was almost entirely over. She picked up the frame and dropped it in the trash bag. She did the same with the wedding album in the closet, not bothering to look inside, and then tied the bag shut.

Sue put the jewelry, including the now-famous cuff links, and cash in her purse. She'd sell the jewelry, including her wedding ring, and invest it back into the bookstore. Sue felt it was only right her past life paid for her new one.

Melba had been teaching her the ropes over the last few months since she'd officially bought the store, and Sue was eager to expand. She and Jameson discussed opening a wall between their businesses so that customers could flow both ways. The stage would be perfect for musicians, visiting authors, and spoken word poets.

Vivien appeared in the doorway, drawing Sue from her rambling thoughts. "Good news. We're all set. You can trust this one. I've arranged for her to sell whatever the new owners want to keep with the property. I told her she could keep her commission rate for any large items she sells on our behalf. Food, clothes, anything else you leave behind will be donated to charity. She'll have any evaluations and donation receipts mailed to us. You'll want those for your taxes."

"Sounds perfect, thank you."

"What else?" Vivien looked around the room. "Oh, you'll sign a few contracts today so she can start the house listing, but everything after that will be done with electronic signatures. At most, we'll have to get a notary signature and mail something back. I know you're motivated to sell, and I told her that, but I also said not to bother you with lowball cheap offers. Her company has a service, and they'll take care of the lawn mowing. Once we leave, there is very little you will have to do."

Sue breathed a sigh of relief. "Thank you for taking care of that. It's a great relief."

"Of course."

Sue grabbed a portable fire safe that contained all her important papers—social security cards, bank info, and copies of Hank's death certificate. She then opened a few drawers and began piling clothes on the floor. "This will be the last of it. Oh, and the guns in the safe. I suppose I can't leave Hank's weapons here. I'd throw them away, but that's probably not good either. I don't want to keep anything of his."

"We'll take them to a gun store and sell them before we leave town," Vivien said. "That way you'll have a receipt that proves you properly disposed of them."

Jameson returned with a duffle bag and grabbed the trash bag. "I'm going to take all the garbage out and put new liners in the bins before we go."

"Thank you." Sue could tell he was trying to help her get through the house as quickly as possible.

Vivien kneeled and started shoving the clothes into the bag. "Just these?"

"Yep." Sue went to the closet and dropped some shirts on the pile, hangers and all.

She then went to open the gun safe in the closet. She put the weapons and ammo into one of Hank's suitcases, along with his paperwork. Then, writing the combination on a sticky note, she affixed it to the door.

"Clothes are done. Jameson is putting them in the car." Vivien touched Sue's shoulder. "What is it?"

"I was thinking that I'm lucky Hank decided to use a hammer and not any of his knives or guns." She gestured to his bag. "He had enough of this crap."

"Let's go sell them, and you can use the profits to buy an entire section of self-help books for empowering women," Vivien suggested. "Or romance novels with alpha women. Whichever he'd hate more."

Sue chuckled.

"I love you, Viv. I don't know where I'd be if it wasn't for you, Lorna, and Heather." Sue rolled her eyes. "And Julia, of course."

"Anything else?" Jameson asked, joining them. His focused expression said he was determined to get this over with for her. "The realtor is waiting for you in the kitchen to sign some papers."

Sue smiled at him.

"What?" he asked.

"I love you," she said. "I'm glad you're here."

At that, his expression softened. He pulled her into his arms and kissed her gently. "I love you, too. And where else would I be but here with you?"

"That's sweet," Vivien interrupted. "Jameson, be a doll and put this bag in the back seat. And be extra careful with it."

He furrowed his brow as he looked at the suitcase.

"I'll go look over the papers for you," Vivien said as an excuse to leave. "I'll have her meet you outside so I can smudge the negative energy out of here before it gets new owners."

"Viv is kind of bossy," Jameson noted.

"She wants to make this as fast as possible for me. Plus, she knows her business with this real estate stuff. I'm lucky to have her." Sue stayed in his arms. "I'm lucky to have you too."

"So dare I ask, what's in the bag?"

"Self-help books and romance novels with strong female leads," Sue answered. "Or they will be. In my purse is a new archway in the wall between our stores. And right now, I'm going to go sign some papers that will give me the rest of what I need for remodeling."

Jameson picked up the suitcase, and they walked out of the house together.

The End

**The Magical Fun Continues!**
**Order of Magic Book 5**
**The Sixth Spell**

GET THE BOOKS!

## The Magical Fun Continues!

Lorna's Story:
Order of Magic Book 1: Second Chance Magic

Vivien's Story:
Order of Magic Book 2: Third Time's a Charm

Heather's Story:
Order of Magic Book 3: The Fourth Power

SECOND CHANCE MAGIC
ORDER OF MAGIC BOOK 1

*Secrets broke her heart... and have now come back
from the grave to haunt her.*

So far, Lorna Addams' forties are not what she
expected. After a very public embarrassment, she
finds it difficult to trust her judgment when it comes
to new friendships and dating. She might be willing
to give love a second chance when she meets the
attractive William Warrick, if only she could come to
terms with what her husband did to her and leave it
in the past.

How is a humiliated empty nest widow supposed
to move on with her life? It's not like she can develop
a sixth sense, séance her ex back, force him to tell her
why and give her closure. Or can she?

THIRD TIME'S A CHARM

ORDER OF MAGIC BOOK 2

*Friends don't let friends séance drunk.*

Vivien Stone lost the love of her life over twenty years ago. Now that she's in her forties with a string of meaningless relationships under her belt, she can't help but pine for what might have been. It doesn't help that she's somewhat psychic and can pretty much predict where a relationship is heading before it even starts.

When she and her best friends find a hidden book of séances, Vivien believes it's the perfect opportunity to talk to her lost love. But things don't go as planned and what was meant to be a romantic reunion takes a turn for the bizarre.

Maybe some things (and people) are better left

buried in the past, and what she really needs has been standing in front of her all along.

THE FOURTH POWER

ORDER OF MAGIC BOOK 3

Heather Harrison sees ghosts. It's not something she brags about. In fact, she wished she didn't. Communicating (or not communicating) with the dead only leads to heartache, and for her it led to a divorce. For the most part, she's happy being single. She's got a good business, close friends, and a slightly overprotective brother. What more does a forty-something woman need?

When her two best friends beg her for help in contacting loved ones, against her better judgment she can't say no to the séance. But some gateways shouldn't be opened, and some meddling spirits shouldn't be stirred...like that of her Grandma who insists she's "found her a nice man".

The supernaturals have come out to play and it's up to this amateur medium to protect herself and her friends before the danger they summoned comes to bite them in the backside.

# ABOUT MICHELLE M. PILLOW

## *New York Times* & *USA TODAY*
## Bestselling Author

Michelle loves to travel and try new things, whether it's a paranormal investigation of an old Vaudeville Theatre or climbing Mayan temples in Belize. She believes life is an adventure fueled by copious amounts of coffee.

Newly relocated to the American South, Michelle is involved in various film and documentary projects with her talented director husband. She is mom to a fantastic artist. And she's managed by a dog and cat who make sure she's meeting her deadlines.

For the most part she can be found wearing pajama pants and working in her office. There may or may not be dancing. It's all part of the creative process.

**Come say hello! Michelle loves talking with readers on social media!**

www.MichellePillow.com

PLEASE TAKE A MOMENT TO SHARE YOUR THOUGHTS BY REVIEWING THIS BOOK.

Thank you to all the wonderful readers who take the time to share your thoughts about the books you love. I can't begin to tell you how important you are when it comes to helping other readers discover the books!

facebook.com/AuthorMichellePillow

twitter.com/michellepillow

instagram.com/michellempillow

bookbub.com/authors/michelle-m-pillow

goodreads.com/Michelle_Pillow

amazon.com/author/michellepillow

youtube.com/michellepillow

pinterest.com/michellepillow

# NEWSLETTER

To stay informed about when a new book in the series installments is released, sign up for updates:

Sign up for Michelle's Newsletter

michellepillow.com/author-updates

CPSIA information can be obtained
at www.ICGtesting.com
Printed in the USA
LVHW111039210821
695815LV00020B/457

9 781625 012623